DON'T SHOOT THE PIANIST

Lew Jackson had made quite a name for himself as a jazz musician but his marriage had failed and his playing had suffered because of it. He found himself managing a seedy jazz club in Battersea which had seen better days. However, a chance to meet a young whizz-kid promoter came his way and Lew persuaded him to put up the money for a jazz festival. But what Lew could not have foreseen was that he would be set up. The local underworld king had plans to use the festival for his own ends and Lew was just a pawn in the game

DON'T SHOOT
THE PIANIST

James Grant

A Lythway Book

CHIVERS PRESS
BATH

First published 1980
by
Judy Piatkus (Publishers) Limited
This Large Print edition published by
Chivers Press
by arrangement with
Judy Piatkus (Publishers)
1982

ISBN 0 85119 854 6

British Library Cataloguing in Publication Data

Grant, James
    Don't shoot the pianist.—Large print ed.
    —(A Lythway book)
    I. Title
    823'.914[F]   PR6057.R/

    ISBN 0–85119–854–6

DON'T SHOOT THE PIANIST

CHAPTER ONE

'Look at it from the punter's point of view. They have the choice of going up west to Ronnie Scott's or coming down here. At Ronnie Scott's they can sit in comfort, eat good food and listen to the best jazz musicians in the world until three o'clock in the morning. Here, in this rat-infested cellar, they have to eat the worst curry this side of Jumbo Patel's takeaway and listen to you singing with Jock Strap and his Two Swingers. If that isn't enough, they have to be out on the street by half-past eleven because we can't get the licence extended. I mean, there's no competition, is there?'

Lew Jackson stared into the bottom of his glass and nodded morosely. 'You're right, Joe. You'd think Ronnie would get the message and pack it in, wouldn't you?'

The door opened and a draught of cold air came down from the street. Joe Nealis turned his head and glanced upwards as a pair of legs appeared at the top of the stairs. 'Oh, Christ,' he said.

'You called?'

'Cut the bloody jokes, Lew. We're in trouble and you know it.'

Lew turned and looked at the legs cautiously negotiating the unlit stairs. The legs were long, black and seemed to go on forever before decency prevailed and the hem of the lady's skirt came into view. 'We could go public,' he suggested.

Joe banged his glass down on to the bar counter with an exasperated snort. 'The lease is due for renewal in two months,' he said. 'We already owe three months' rent to Reeder. We have an overdraft the size of the National Debt and all you can do is make jokes. Let's talk sense, shall we?'

Lew turned away from the legs and nodded slowly. 'Sorry, mate. It's not a very good prospect, is it?'

'Reeder will want to put the rent up at renewal.'

'He can stick it if he does.'

'Are you going to tell him that?'

Lew scowled and glared across the room at the owner of the long legs and short skirt who was now in full view and striding across the unswept wooden floor. 'No, I suppose not,' he said. He managed to form a smile, aiming it in the general direction of the tall, thin, black girl who grinned cheerfully back at him. 'Early tonight, Honey. Keen to get down to business?'

'That's another thing,' Joe said. 'We can do without her and her kind. Given the place a bad name they have.'

'I would've thought that was impossible. What're you drinking, Honey?'

'Coke, please, Lew.'

'There, you see, Joe. None of the hard stuff for the lady. Don't you wish we had a few more like her?'

Joe glowered at the girl. 'A few more like her and I'd have my coronary now and save all the trouble of waiting until the hospital's full of flu victims and dockers with bad backs.' Nealis finished his beer and sat grimly refusing to smile at either the black girl or his partner. Nealis, a spidery-thin man with pale skin and gingery hair, had bright blue eyes which blinked rapidly when he was excited or irritable. They were blinking now with machine-gun-like fervour. Trying to talk business with Lew was like trying to strike a match on a jelly – not difficult if you knew the secret but bloody impossible if you didn't. After thirty years, Joe Nealis still didn't have the secret.

Lew Jackson wandered round to the back of the bar and snapped the ring on a can of Coca-Cola. He looked for a clean glass, failed to find one, and raised an enquiring eyebrow at the girl whose smile broadened as she took the can and raised it in the air. 'Cheers,' she said.

While he was behind the bar Lew reached for his and Joe's glasses and refilled them. He glanced round the room as he waited for the beer to reach the regulation level in the first glass. The club looked awful when it was empty, he decided. Not that it looked very startling full,

3

but at least a press of sweaty bodies and carefully placed artificial lights hid some of the peeling paint, torn upholstery and general squalor. The club, officially the South Bank Jazz Club, belonged to him and Joe. They had acquired the lease at the end of the fifties when, for the first, last and only time in their lives they'd had a few pounds in the bank and, apparently, a considerable future with their band. The band, Lew Jackson's Southern Syncopaters, had thrived briefly during the trad jazz boom that spawned a dozen bands like theirs – Kenny Ball, Acker Bilk, Alex Welsh, Freddy Randall and scores more that everyone had long forgotten together with the men who played in them. The club, Lew's south-of-the-river answer to Ronnie Scott's club in Frith Street, had seemed like a good idea at the time, but the fifties gave way to the sixties and suddenly jazz bands were old hat, particularly bands of that ilk.

Lew stood his glass on the bar, slid Joe's under the tap, knocked the lever over and watched the beer pour into the glass, all bubbles and froth. Joe had been the band's drummer and, as he'd been a non-drinker in those days, he'd also been the band bus driver, an economy measure that had helped matters a little. It hadn't prevented the inevitable when the band folded one night after a particularly disastrous booking in a Middlesbrough dance hall. The hall had suddenly filled with about a thousand screaming, pubescent girls who seemed to think Lew and his band were old enough to be their fathers, which they were; and worse musicians than the guitar-ridden rock group playing opposite them, which they weren't.

He pushed Joe's glass across the bar and lifted his own, draining half of it in a single swallow. He turned, belched lightly, and as he did so caught a glimpse of himself in the yellowing mirror on the wall behind the glass shelves at the back of the bar. He was a man of medium height but recently added weight had given him an oddly pear-shaped physique. He peered more closely at the reflection in the mirror. The bags under his eyes looked worse than ever but as he'd had them since he was fifteen they were nothing to worry about. The wrinkles were more recent and so was the greying hair around his ears. He prodded a finger into his cheek, then took it out and watched as the flesh took a long, long time to retain its original position. He decided he looked sixty, felt seventy and, since he was only forty-six, clearly it was high time he did something about it.

He considered his waistline bulge exaggerated by the light blue suit with pale yellow window-pane check. Loud suits, mostly horse-blanket check in unlikely colour combinations, had been standard dress since he had reached his twenty-first birthday which had coincided with his fourth anniversary in the business. In need of some gimmick, and as funny hats had been taken up by everyone else, he had tried a wildly-patterned suit. It had looked good then, hung as it had been on a slim body. Over the years the suits had stayed flamboyant but the body had thickened.

'Here.'

He turned to see Joe proffering a packet of cigarettes. Lew reached for one, changed his mind and shook his head. 'No, thanks, I'm giving them up.'

'Again?'

'Yes.' He picked up the remains of the glass of beer and poured it into the slop tray. 'This too.'

'Christ,' Joe said. 'You'll be giving up fucking next.'

'I might at that.'

There was a muffled shriek of laughter from the tall, black, girl.

Lew glared at her. 'Anyway, what the hell are you doing in here at six o'clock? We don't open until eight.'

The girl came along the bar and leaned forward, giving Lew an extensive view inside her blouse at her small, bra-less breasts. 'I need a favour, Lew.'

Lew took his eyes away from her bosom, which he'd seen at much closer range anyway, and looked at her face. The girl was about

6

twenty-six, had been using the club as a centre for hustling johns for five years and had never given any trouble. She was Jamaican, had come to England and got a job in Woolworth's intent on saving enough money to bring over her family from Port Antonio, and then had taken a sharp lesson in elementary economics. The lesson was that at the rate at which Woolies were paying her, by the time she got the family over to England the youngest, her little brother, Winston, would be eligible for his old-age pension. Needing a faster method of earning money she took a hint from a spotty girl on the adjacent counter and tried a couple of evenings of amateur hooking outside the Red Lion at the bottom of Putney High Street. The results, while not spectacular, gave her ambitions some hope of fulfilment. She took a few quick lessons in man-management, handed in her check dress and became a full-time whore. Now, although her little brother had been in England long enough to speak with a raw, South London accent and get his name on a cluster of charge sheets at the Upper Richmond Road nick, Honey showed no inclination to stop hustling. She liked the money, now that she could spend it on herself and, unusually, she still liked sex enough to want it as often as possible. Lew didn't know her name – she'd arrived with a ready-made nickname, the Honeydripper, and, apart from shortening it to Honey, he'd let it go

7

at that.

'What sort of favour?' he asked. 'I can just about manage the price of a telephone call if you promise to pay it back before midnight.'

'Not money, Lew. Can I borrow your car?'

'The car?'

'Please.'

'I suppose so. Planning on going after the carriage trade?'

'Pardon?'

'Never mind. Tell me if you want to; don't if you don't.' He fumbled in his pockets for the keys to the five-year-old Granada standing in the narrow alleyway behind the club.

'I didn't know you could drive,' Joe put in.

'I can't. Dwight's going to drive me.'

'Dwight?'

'My brother.'

'Can he drive?'

'He drives a bus for London Transport.'

'So he can't drive.'

'Pardon?'

'Never mind. Sure, here you are.' Lew tossed the keys across to the girl who caught them and whisked them out of sight into her shoulder-bag.

'Thanks, Lew. I couldn't get all the stuff I need over to Hampstead without a car.'

'Stuff?'

'You know, music, Winston's guitar, Dwight's conga drum.'

'Guitar? Conga drum? What're you up to?'

The girl glanced away in embarrassment then shrugged her shoulders, her tiny breasts doing a little jig inside the unlimiting confines of her blouse. 'I'm auditioning.'

'Auditioning,' Lew and Joe said together.

'For a recording contract.'

Lew looked at Joe who blinked several times. 'Recording contract,' Lew said, realizing he was starting to sound like a pale echo as he kept repeating the Honeydripper's words.

'I met a man last week, at a party. Afterwards he said he liked the way I sang and he'd let me audition for his record company.'

'Hey, come on, Honey. You're a big girl now. That one went out with casting couches.'

'Oh, no, Lew. He does have a record company. I've seen him on the telly. His name's Eddie Lester. He has a white Rolls-Royce,' she added as if that settled the matter of identification and authenticity.

'Never heard of him,' Lew said.

'I have,' Joe put in. 'Made a pile of money selling army greatcoats to trendy misfits and drop-outs in the sixties. Shifted his money into Italian sports cars – he had the concession for Maseratis for a while. Then he took on a couple of pop groups, bought out a record company and suddenly became very rich. Got himself on the telly as a talent competition judge. Lives in Hampstead, owns a farm in Wiltshire, a villa in

9

Estoril, has a wife and three kids, two spaniels and a hamster called William.'

Lew had listened with his mouth slowly opening wider. 'Where did you get all that?'

'This week's *TV Times*.'

'I never knew you read anything but *Jazz Journal*.'

'I'm trying to broaden my education.'

'So it seems.' Lew turned back to the girl. 'I didn't know you could sing, Honey.'

The girl smiled. 'Didn't think you'd be interested, Lew.'

He held out his hand. 'Let me have the keys back,' he said.

Honey's face dropped. 'Oh, Lew.'

'No, don't worry, you're still on. I'll drive you.'

'You will? Why . . . what about the club?'

'Joe can manage, can't you mate?'

'I usually do.'

'Anyway, I'd like to hear you sing.'

'Thanks, Lew.'

'What time have you to be there?'

'Eight.'

'Hampstead, you said.'

'East Heath Road. He has a studio at his house.'

'Okay. Tell your brothers to be here at half-past seven. No, make that quarter-past, we don't want to keep the man waiting.'

'Thanks, Lew,' Honey said again and leaned

forward to deposit a hasty, damp kiss on his cheek before striding across the floor towards the stairs.

'What are you up to?' Joe asked.

'Up to?'

'Don't come the innocent with me.'

'This Eddie Lester. He's not short of a bob or two.'

'You can say that again.'

'So. We're broke, he's flush. A man who's put money into army surplus, flash cars, pop groups and the record business might not be averse to putting a few shekels into something a bit more uplifting.'

'Like what?'

Lew waved an arm. 'Like a jazz festival.'

'Oh my God. Not that one again. I thought you'd given that idea up.'

'It's a good idea.'

'A good idea for who? Let's face it, you're no George Wein.'

'The only difference between me and George Wein is that I'm broke. Apart from the fact that I play piano better than he does.'

'Forget the festival, Lew. If you can con this Lester character out of a quid or two, put it into the club.'

'A quid or two? If he's got all you say he has he'll be good for a few thousand.'

'Lew.'

'I'm not going to rob the man. Just put a

11

business proposition to him. He didn't get where he is today by not listening to business propositions.'

'He didn't get where he is today putting money into half-assed jazz festivals.'

'Balls,' Lew said genially. He went behind the bar and poured himself a large whisky.

'I thought you'd given it up.'

'The beer, not the hard stuff. Beer's fattening.'

'That right?' Nealis looked down at his own rail-thin frame. 'Haven't noticed it.'

'That's because you were a late starter. Not weaned on it like me.'

'There's something bothering me about Honey's story,' Joe said, after a moment.

'What?'

'What kind of trick was she turning for this Lester guy?'

'Meaning?'

'She never sang when she was in bed with me.'

'Me neither,' Lew agreed. 'Maybe it's his hang-up. Makes 'em sing while he fucks 'em. Takes all sorts, you know.' He drained his glass, came around the bar and laid an arm across Nealis's thin shoulders. 'Manage without me?'

'Like I said, I usually do.'

'Don't know what I'd do without you, mate.'

'Neither do I, Lew, neither do I.'

'Right. I'll slide off home, have a shave and

12

put on my snake-charmer's outfit.' He walked to the stairs and was half-way up them before Joe spoke again.

'Lew.'

'What?'

'Don't do anything illegal, will you?'

Lew Jackson turned, his face, in the half-light, a picture of innocent surprise. 'Illegal? Me? Where do you get evil thoughts like that, Joe?'

'Knowing you for thirty bloody years, that's where.'

Lew blew an indelicate raspberry and went out of the door into the street.

He had a flat in the basement of a house in Esmond Street and walked there in five minutes. The flat had two rooms plus a tiny bathroom and an even smaller kitchen. The previous occupant had been something fairly junior in a fine arts establishment and had decorated and furnished the flat in a plain, almost stark, style to set off the paintings he brought home from work. It seemed that the idea of bringing such things out of the gallery was entirely his own and when his employers found out about it harsh words were spoken. Lew moved into the flat the day the young man moved into an open prison in Hertfordshire. He bought the furnishings for a song because at that time he was living in a furnished flat in East Sheen.

13

He had tried house-owning once, during his brief second marriage. His wife had insisted on it, assuming that responsibilities were all that were needed to keep him on the straight and narrow. Her assumption was wrong, as she discovered when the building society obtained a possession order for non-payment of mortgage and chose to implement it while Lew was playing a gig at the Humberstone Country Club near Grimsby. She made three desperate telephone calls to Lew during the two-week engagement, one in the hope he would tell her it was all a dreadful mistake, the next to beg him to come home and sort things out, the third to threaten to leave him. Immune to all three calls, Lew returned home after the job was over to find the locks had been changed on the doors of the house in Wallington and his wife had gone to stay with her sister in Godalming. That had been eight years ago and, as far as he knew, she was still there. Since then he had lived in a succession of flats and this one, undoubtedly the best of the bunch, seemed like being home for quite some time. He had done little to personalize it – a few books and records, and on the walls where the previous occupier had hung works by Matisse and Monet he had stuck some 1930s' fliers for the Savoy Ballroom in New York. The lack of personalization wasn't deliberate, it simply never occurred to him that a flat or a house should be treated as anything

14

other than somewhere to go when nothing was happening anywhere else. It was also handy to have somewhere to take an occasional lady friend who didn't have suitable accommodation of her own. Not that he ever let one instal herself for more than a one-night stand or weekend gig. It wasn't their presence he objected to but the fact that, after more than two or three consecutive days in the place, they started polishing things and putting the knives and forks into separate compartments in the cutlery drawer in his miniscule kitchen.

He washed, shaved more carefully than usual and splashed on some pungent after-shave. With his face twisted in a grimace as the liquid bit into a couple of nicks he'd made in his chin, he rummaged through his wardrobe. After some thought he put on a purple and green check suit which looked slightly less hideous than it sounded. The suit had been part of his old on-stage image and he completed the picture of a man with unusual dress sense by putting on a bright, broad, floral-patterned tie in yellow and red. Looking at the result in the wardrobe mirror he came to the conclusion that Eddie Lester couldn't fail to be impressed. He tossed a mental coin between a pair of brown and white shoes and dark brown suede slip-ons which won because they didn't need cleaning. Glancing at his watch he decided against a cup of coffee, hoping that Eddie Lester would spring

15

something stronger. On his way to the door he kicked against a little pile of dust and spent matches and swore mildly. He never cleaned or tidied the flat, relying instead on the irregular visits of an old crone who 'did' for him, supposedly one day every week. The old girl had a decidedly faulty memory, one result of which was that she would sometimes forget to come for several weeks on end. Another effect of her memory was that she would often sweep the accumulated debris into neat little piles, then go home leaving them for Lew to stumble into in the dark, thus re-spreading them all over the room.

It was seven o'clock when he left the flat, and when he reached the club Honey was waiting for him with her two brothers, both taller and thinner than she was. The youngest, Winston, clasped his guitar to his chest as if afraid he might be asked to leave it behind. Dwight had his conga drum slung from a gaudy strap which crossed his chest like a bandolier.

'Hey, hey, the band's all here,' Lew said cheerfully as he opened the car doors for them all. He started the engine and drove out into the main road, past the front of the club with its tatty sign proclaiming the night's attraction, Harry Betts with the Joe Nealis Trio. 'Harry bloody Betts,' Lew murmured under his breath. 'What an asshole.'

'Pardon?' Honey said.

16

'Nothing, darling. Just thinking about my past. Let's forget it and think about the future instead.' He began to whistle a few bars of *There'll Be Some Changes Made*, then stopped and asked what Honey planned to sing at her audition.

'*Can't Stop Rafta Now.*'

'Oh,' he said blankly.

'It goes like this, Lew.' She began to sing, her voice soft and husky, the words an almost unintelligible jumble that mixed English with her native patois. Her brothers, sitting in the back of the car, joined in and after a few bars Lew picked up the tune and began to whistle counterpoint to the melody. To his surprise he found it was a pleasant song and, even more surprising, Honey sang well. Maybe Eddie Lester was a smart lad, after all, he thought. Well, the smarter the better because the idea for the jazz festival was one that needed a good business brain to see the opportunities it presented. All things considered, Lew decided, it looked like being a highly promising evening.

Back somewhere near the beginning of time, his father had entertained vague notions about Lew going into business and making a future wheeling and dealing in the City. His father had been an accountant with a City firm and had been most disappointed to discover his only son had no head for figures. Unfortunately that discovery wasn't made until after Lew had

17

entered a very upper-crust school on the outskirts of Godalming which had produced several captains of industry and a Prime Minister or two.

A year after he had started there Lew had wandered into a dance hall in Woking, seen and heard a traditional jazz band and, at the end of the evening, had gone up to talk to the band. Most of them were too tired, too drunk or too set on picking the best of the available talent to talk to a sixteen-year-old kid who thought he could play the piano and sing. The band's drummer took pity on him, let him play and sing and realized there was a lot of talent in the boy. The drummer, Joe Nealis, although only a couple of years older than Lew, stoically endured a mild case of hero-worship from the young public schoolboy.

When the band moved on Lew went back to school, practised his piano-playing and singing, and studied not at all. Six months later the band returned to Woking with a very drunk pianist who fell off his stool at the end of the first set. Joe spotted Lew, had a word with the band leader who was sufficiently pissed off to have hired Charlie Kunz had he been available, and the young man was taken on for the rest of the evening.

When the band left for Southampton the next morning Lew went with them, sending a note to his father who wrote an apoplectic letter back which resulted in a four-year gap in communication between them. At the end of those four years Lew had his own band, was making records, appearing on the radio and even on the telly where his slightly upper-crust accent had endeared him to the BBC hierarchy which had yet to be infiltrated by trendy left-wing activists with carefully cultivated working-class accents and thick-knit, roll-neck pullovers. And he also, with Joe, owned the club. His father relented, came to visit, admitted to having been a long-time devotee of Bix Beiderbecke and even offered to keep the club's books.

It was about then that Lew began to harbour delusions of grandeur, seeing the promotion of concerts as more lucrative than playing them. The sudden onrush of rock groups took the ground from under him and the death of his father removed a business brain on which he could rely. Since then his movements had been generally downwards but he had never relinquished the hope that a way up might present itself. A recording company was one dream but that needed capital and had a low return, at least as far as jazz was concerned. Radio or TV was another route but he had rapidly discovered that talent came a poor second to knowing the right people. Concert promotion was another avenue and the most feasible. It needed capital but not too much, and the returns, if all went well, could be good if not great.

The problem was the capital. He'd never had much and now he had none at all. He'd tried persuading various people to back him but had always failed for a variety of reasons. He had a feeling this time he wouldn't. Eddie Lester was obviously a sharp lad, into pop music and recording, into quick ways to make a bob or two. He could very easily prove to be the very man Lew had been looking for. He felt a mild twinge of guilt at the realization that he was implying Joe wasn't the ideal partner. To a great extent that was true. He was as straight as a die, honest as the day was long and he was a competent, if unspectacular, musician. But he lacked the spark needed to push them up out of the rut. If Joe had been a bit more go-ahead, more dynamic, he would have been an ideal partner, the way Pete King was to Ronnie Scott.

Lew shrugged off the thought. Joe wasn't Pete King any more than he was Ronnie Scott. He brightened at the thought that, if he could get the festival off the ground, make it work and break even, then both Pete and Ronnie would have to watch out – the Lew Jackson–Joe Nealis bandwagon might very well grind them into the ground.

CHAPTER TWO

'What's next?' Reeder asked.

'Jumbo Patel's takeaway in Weimar Street.'

'He's regular, isn't he?'

'As clockwork.'

'Up ten per cent.'

'Yes, Mr Reeder.'

'Next.'

'The South Bank Jazz Club.'

Reeder's face wrinkled in mild distaste. 'Haven't they seen the light yet?'

'Seems not, Mr Reeder.'

'Regular?'

'Three months behind, Mr Reeder.'

'Three months? Bleeding hell. What do you think I'm running here? A bleeding benevolent society?'

'No, Mr Reeder. It was Mr Toner said we shouldn't lean on them.'

'Sid?'

'Yes, Mr Reeder.'

'All right, I'll talk to him. Sid never does anything without a reason. Next.'

'Marcus and Aubrey, the hairdressers in Quill Lane.'

'Bleeding fruits. Up twenty per cent.'

'Yes, Mr Reeder.'

Jack Reeder liked to refer to himself as a

21

villain. His use of the word bore testimony to an instinctive awareness of the nature of language. The word 'villain' had a ring to it, it made him sound like an old-fashioned buccaneer, a man who would rob the rich, give to the poor and save a damsel in distress at the drop of a wimple. In fact he was a narrow-minded, sadistic, thoroughly evil little man. He had no morals, no scruples, no friends and more enemies than he liked to think about on the few occasions he risked going anywhere without the two bodyguards who were at this moment propping up the wall in the passage outside his office door. Reeder's kingdom was the area of London bounded to the north by the river, to the south by the Kingston by-pass, and which lay between Vauxhall Bridge and the perimeter fence at Heathrow. The airport itself was, of course, common territory, open to all but, by convention entered only after discussion between Reeder and other territory bosses. In the area he controlled very little took place he didn't know about and get a cut from. Illegal gambling, even some of the perfectly legal betting shop business, went through his hands. He either owned or had an interest in drinking clubs, blue movie houses, strip clubs, massage parlours, several used car lots, a couple of pubs the big brewers hadn't been able to get their hands on, most of the prostitution, all the drug-pushing, very nearly all the breaking and entering and certainly all the heavy jobs. Every bank, jeweller, post office, supermarket or payroll job was down to him or, on the few occasions he was obliged to watch his step, to a neighbouring villain brought in on a commission basis. On top of all that he ran a neat line in protection on most of the business premises in the area, except those he owned. Where he owned the property he simply levied regular, heavy rent increases on the principle that threats of setting fire to, or otherwise wrecking, property he owned himself were likely to fall on incredulous ears.

The rent review session ended and the room was emptied of everyone except Reeder. He waited until the door closed before he climbed out of his chair. Standing up, Jack Reeder wasn't much taller than when he was sitting down. He was very wide but his bulk looked hard and muscular, not at all podgy. He had thinning black hair combed forward to hide a bald patch, which gave him a faintly Napoleonic appearance. It was an appearance he cultivated, unaware that his detractors considered it made him look like a somewhat truncated version of Mick McManus.

He stumped across to the window, glared down into the street and then, when he was sure that everyone, apart from the guards outside the door, was far enough away not to hear anything he went back to the desk and dialled the number of his right-hand man, Sid Toner.

'Sid?' he enquired when a non-committal grunt echoed in his ear.

'Yes, Jack.'

'The South Bank Jazz Club.'

'What about it?'

'They're three months behind with the rent.'

'I know.'

'What are we doing about it?'

'Nothing.'

'Nothing?'

'Nothing.'

There was silence before Reeder tried again. 'Sid, it's bad for the image. Others might take the hint.'

'We risk it.'

'We do?'

'Jack, trust me. There's a reason.'

Reeder sighed. 'Okay, Sid. If you say so.' He replaced the telephone but not before Toner had broken the connection. Reeder was pleased he'd ensured no one else had overheard the conversation. It wouldn't have done a lot for his standing, him having to talk to Sid like that, but the hard fact of the matter was that, while Jack Reeder had muscle and no scruples about using it, he relied on Sid Toner's brains more than anyone knew and more than he liked. He thought for a moment about the jazz club and the two dead-beats who ran it, then shrugged the thought from his mind. If Sid Toner said

24

there was a reason, then reason there was. As for trusting Sid, that went without saying. After all, if it came to the crunch Sid knew, and Jack knew he knew, that any sign of double-dealing would be dealt with sharply. Sid would receive the same treatment a couple of other former cronies had had meted out to them. However brainy Sid was, there wasn't all that much a man could do to think himself out of being concreted into the foundations of a multi-storey car park in Catford.

Jack Reeder crossed to the door, opened it and beckoned to one of the heavyweights. 'Get the car,' he ordered. He decided it was time he had a look at some of the property he owned and it wouldn't do any harm to start with the South Bank Jazz Club. He wondered who would be appearing there. He tried to remember the names of some jazz musicians and after several moments' hard thinking came up with Louis Armstrong and Sammy Davis. As far as he knew the first was dead and he wasn't all that sure if the second really was a jazz musician. One thing he was sure about, because he'd seen him on the telly, Davis was American and black. As far as Reeder was concerned all black Americans were either sprinters, boxers or jazz musicians. He puzzled over Davis for a few more moments, and by the time his car arrived he'd decided that he'd been wrong about him. He wasn't a jazz musician, he was a boxer. Light heavyweight, probably. Spades usually were.

'Where to, Mr Reeder?' his driver asked when he was settled into the back seat of the Mercedes.

'Montserrat Road, the jazz club.'

'Yes, Mr Reeder.' There was a note of surprise in the driver's voice. But he wasn't paid to question his boss. As the Mercedes turned on to Putney High Street it passed a rusting Granada driven by a white man with a very pretty black girl in the front passenger seat and two young black men in the back. Reeder didn't notice them and they didn't notice Reeder. There was no reason why any of them should have done so.

CHAPTER THREE

'He's going to do it, mate, he's going to do it!'

'Who's going to do what?'

'Honey's lover-boy is going to back the jazz festival. The little darling must have got him all of a tremble.'

'Slow down, Lew,' Nealis said. 'Are you trying to tell me that this boy genius, this ace promoter, this superstar hustler is going to put money into your cock-eyed venture?'

'Too true, old buddy. Anyway, he's not such a boy. He must be thirty-five if he's a day.'

'Even that's a bit early for senility to have set in.'

'Come on, Joe, the festival isn't a bad idea. It can make us all a few quid and also get you and me back into the swing of things again.'

'But a jazz festival in Battersea. It doesn't sound right, Lew.'

'George Wein and Andy Hudson are holding them at Ally Pally. They have them at Edinburgh, Chichester, Bolton, Kendal even. Damn it all, they even held one in Middlesbrough a few years back and you know what happened to us up there.'

'I prefer not to think about the low points in my life.'

'Stop being bloody miserable and pour me a drink.'

Nealis was behind the bar at the club. The room, otherwise empty of people, was littered with the usual debris of a night's drinking, the pungent smell of curry blending uneasily with stale cigarette smoke. He poured out a scotch for Lew and opened a bottle of tonic water for himself.

'Good night?' Lew asked.

'We've had worse. Had a party in from Guildford Law College. Drank less than last week's rugby club outing but made less noise, thank God.'

'What was the ageing genius of the tenor saxophone like tonight?'

'Harry? Not bad. I've heard him play worse.'

'I'm not sure whether that's a commendation or not.'

'Neither am I.'

'Right. Let me tell you the gory details of my little coup,' Lew said. 'Eddie Lester will put up the loot. Ten thousand up front to let me get started booking artists, the hall, all the odds and ends.'

'Hall? I thought the grand plan was for an outdoor bash in Battersea Park.'

'It was but he vetoed that. Wants it at Putney Town Hall.'

'Why there?'

'He wants to record the entire proceedings. That way we get two bites at the cherry.'

'Any other changes to the master plan?'

Lew took a large sip from his drink. 'None. Everything else stays the way it was. I have a free hand on booking artists, the whole of the artistic side is my responsibility. He handles the recording and, of course, pays the bills until the money starts rolling in.'

'Then what?'

'Then what, what?'

'What happens to the bills after the money starts rolling in?'

'We pay as we go. Divvy up the proceeds afterwards and bob's your uncle.'

'We all walk into the sunset with a thousand angels singing the *Hallelujah Chorus*.'

'Joe, try a smile, mate. We're on our way.'

'Jack Reeder was in here tonight.'

'Here?'

'Yes.'

'What did he want?'

'He didn't say. That's what's worrying me.'

'What happened?'

'Nothing. He came in just after you floated off with Putney's answer to Diana Ross. Sat here until we closed, with his two gorillas, drinking Bloody Marys until I thought they'd come out of his ears.'

'Did he like the show?'

'I watched him while we were playing. Apart from tapping his foot in waltz time it didn't seem too painful an experience for him.'

'He said nothing?'

'After the last set he asked me to introduce him to Harry.'

'And?'

'He seemed disappointed Harry was Scottish, seemed he didn't know there were any jazz musicians up there.'

'There aren't all that many, all the good ones are down here. He said nothing about the lease?'

'No, so I didn't either.'

'That's all right then.'

'I'm not sure about that. Maybe he was casing the place to decide how much he could jack up the rent.'

'I keep telling you, Joe, stop worrying. By the

time the festival's over we'll be able to pay whatever he asks, unless we decide to move on to better things.'

'Always the optimist.'

'One of us has to be.'

'Your optimism brings out the pessimist in me.'

'Now who's making the jokes?'

'Who's joking?'

Lew finished his drink and stretched his arms above his head. 'Right, it's past two. Time I went to beddy-byes. Mustn't keep the little lady waiting.'

'Who's the lucky girl?'

'Sarcastic bastard. The Honeydripper of course. Thought we might as well end the evening in style.'

'Try asking her to sing with your weight on top of her.'

Jackson patted his stomach. 'This'll be gone soon, don't worry about that. I'm going on a diet, no bread, no potatoes, no beer and all the fucking I can get. That should keep me thin.'

'It should keep part of you thin, anyway.'

'Lock up carefully,' Lew said as he headed for the stairs.

'There's nothing here worth stealing, apart from my drums and I'm not all that sure about them.'

'Jesus, you take a lot of pleasing, Joe.'

'That's what all the ladies say.'

'Balls.'

On the stairs Lew turned and leaned over the balustrade, which creaked ominously. 'Reeder didn't say anything else, then?'

Joe Nealis thought for a moment. 'He asked me if I'd ever heard of a boxer called Sammy Davis.'

'What did you say?'

'I told him there used to be a light heavyweight of that name in Southwark. That seemed to please him, except he thought he should have been an American as well.'

'Maybe he's going mad. It happened to Al Capone.'

'Couldn't be from the same cause.'

'Oh?'

'Rumour has it that our esteemed landlord can't get it up any more.'

'It comes to us all in the end.'

'Speaking from experience?'

'I'm leaving before the tone of this conversation falls below its usual abysmal standard.'

Alone in the club, Joe Nealis slowly sipped his drink, then began his nightly tour, checking that everything was turned or switched off and the fire exit doors were locked. As he made his rounds he thought about Lew and his ambitions. They hadn't been apparent for some time. Joe had assumed, hoped, that his partner had given them up and settled for the life they'd drifted into. The early days seemed so long ago in his memory, it was as if he and Lew were two other people. He had been almost nineteen, even thinner than he was now, full of nervous energy, a good if unimaginative drummer and firmly convinced he would end up rich, happy, married and with a houseful of kids. Out of that little lot of ambition he had managed only one. He was married but even that wasn't what it had been.

He switched his mind on to Lew and the time he had first met him. Lew had been slim, quite pleasant-looking, a good piano-player and singer, very enthusiastic and bloody impossible. Now, thirty years on, he still had most of those characteristics. The slimness had gone but despite that he hadn't lost his looks, at least on the few occasions he got a straight seven hours' sleep. He was still a good piano-player and his singing had improved as his voice matured. His attitude that evening showed he could still be enthusiastic, although usually about crazy things. As for his being impossible, Joe shook his head and grinned humourlessly. If he had been impossible in the early days the word hadn't been devised to describe him now.

Joe went up the stairs and out into Montserrat Road, locked the door of the club and walked to where he had parked his car in Atney Road. He was well on his way home to his flat in Fawe Park Road, opposite Wandsworth Park, before he could push aside the nagging thought that, despite his casual treatment of the subject, Jack Reeder's presence at the club that night had had an ulterior motive. It worried him and it would probably have worried him even more if he'd known that even Jack Reeder hadn't known the reason for the visit. Reeder's sudden interest in the South Bank Jazz Club had been precipitated by Sid Toner's unusual attitude towards the club and its owners, and for the time being Toner was keeping the reason for his interest very much to himself.

As for Lew Jackson, he wasn't interested in his partner's worries or his landlord's peculiarities, and he certainly wasn't interested in Sid Toner whom he'd never met anyway. As he and the Honeydripper rolled and groaned and sweated on the sagging bed in Lew's basement flat he couldn't keep from the forefront of his mind the fact that his long-held dream was about to come true. His very own jazz festival was about to hit South London with a force which would rock it to its foundations. He'd been thinking about it since festivals had become such an important part of the British jazz scene in the mid seventies. He knew the way he wanted this one to go and he knew who he wanted for it. That was the only possible trouble with the deal. He hadn't told Joe, but Eddie Lester had made another condition to his financial involvement. The festival had to be held over the Bank Holiday weekend at the end of August. It was less than two months away and it didn't leave very much time for anything, least of all for being too particular about the big names he would need to attract the punters.

He realized his thinking was getting the better of his actions and began to pump away at the black girl's co-operative body. When he came he rolled over on to his back without bothering to see if she had got anything out of their exertions. She hadn't, but she didn't much care as her mind, too, was on other things.

'Was I good, Lew?' she asked.

'Of course you were, Honey. Best lay in Putney, as I tell all my friends.'

'No, not that, my singing. Was I good tonight?'

Lew reached for a cigarette and lit it before remembering he'd given up smoking. He blew smoke at the ceiling, deciding to give it up in the morning instead. He thought about the audition he'd had to sit through before he could get Eddie Lester alone. Honey hadn't been at all bad, and her brothers' accompaniment had been far from amateurish. 'Yes, you were,' he told the girl. 'Is that the only kind of music you sing?'

'Mostly.'

'Tell you what. Come down to the club tomorrow and we'll have a run through a few standards, see how you shape up with them.'

'Oh, Lew, will you let me sing at the club?'

'We'll see.'

'Oh, Lew.' She clambered on top of him and began to kiss him with considerably more enthusiasm than she'd shown earlier.

After a moment Lew realized he would be busy the next day with his preparation for the festival. The Honeydripper would have to wait until he had some spare time. He was about to tell her but by then she was working her way downwards over his stomach so he decided to wait until she'd finished what she was obviously leading up to. He raised his head to watch and frowned at the sight of his stomach. He really would have to go on to the diet he'd kidded Joe about. If he went on this way it wouldn't be just his shoelaces he'd be losing sight of. The Honeydripper reached her target and went to work with all the expertise her five years on the game had taught her.

Later, having decided that, fair being fair, she wouldn't make any charges for her services, she let herself out of Lew's flat to walk home through the deserted streets. She didn't notice the man in the car in Esmond Street who watched her leave. As soon as the girl was out of sight he climbed out of the car and went to the telephone kiosk on the corner. When the telephone was answered the man reported the result of his night's surveillance.

'Okay,' Sid Toner told him. 'Pack it in now

and get some sleep. Be here at nine and I'll have another little job for you.'

'Right, Mr Toner,' the man said, tactfully refraining from mentioning it was already past four o'clock.

In his expensively, and very tastefully, furnished house in Wimbledon, Sid Toner replaced the telephone and lay back on the pillow, staring at the ceiling which was dappled with light from the moon shining in through the windows. Beside him, his wife stirred in her sleep. The telephone hadn't disturbed her. Very little did, which made her an ideal wife for a villain like Sid Toner. Never asked questions, never even wondered where all the money came from. She had her drawbacks though, Sid thought, as his mind dwelt on the black whore. The thought of the girl began to arouse him and he reached out a hand and rested it on his wife's buttocks. She turned on to her back, her mouth open, and began to snore gently. Toner's desire faded and after a few moments he turned on his side, closed his eyes and drifted off to sleep.

CHAPTER FOUR

In an era when about half the police force looked like bank managers and the other half like refugees from the city's sewers, Detective-Chief Superintendent George Blackstone was an anachronism. He really looked like a copper. He was tall, above the old regulation height, which put him a head above many of his younger colleagues who had crept in after the height had been reduced to a level which, in Blackstone's opinion, had opened up the force to dwarfs, midgets and limbo dancers. He had expressed this view on more than one occasion in the hearing of the press, which delighted them because they thought it was a joke, and caused desperation among his superiors who were, for the most part, of the bank manager variety, because they knew Blackstone never made jokes.

He sat now in his office, his heavy, ribbed face set in a scowl, his neck pulled down into thickly muscled shoulders, his hands resting on the desk like furry animals on either side of a piece of paper sent down to him by the Collator who was forever sending down such things. Blackstone didn't really approve of Collators, computers and colleges from which most of his colleagues seemed to have sprung. He'd learned his trade on the streets and in the alleys of the capital and he disapproved of short-cuts learned from books or machines. Nevertheless he had to admit, grudgingly, that the Collator did turn up the occasional titbit of information worth seeing, even if he was a college-bred midget with a penchant for wearing suede jackets and cashmere pullovers. It looked as if this particular piece of paper was one such gem of potential usefulness. The trouble was, Blackstone couldn't quite see what it all added up to.

The document informed him that during the past few weeks certain specialists had disappeared from their usual haunts and hadn't surfaced anywhere else. Recently, things had been very quiet on his patch and, while that seemed to please everyone else at the nick, it worried him. Jack Reeder and Sid Toner did a lot of things – treading the straight and narrow wasn't one of them.

Blackstone leaned back in his chair which lodged a small protest with a groan. He stared at the wall and the back of the head of his sergeant who, aware of the signs, kept his head low over his papers in an attempt to become invisible.

'Something's up,' Blackstone said.

The sergeant sighed and put down his well-chewed ballpoint. 'Yes, sir?'

'Have you read this?'

'Yes, sir.'

'Something's up,' the big man repeated.

'Yes, sir.'

Silence reigned for a few moments and the sergeant cautiously began to scribble meaningless little symbols in the margin of the top sheet of paper on his overflowing desk in the faint hope that Blackstone would manage without him. It wasn't to be.

'Come on, Green,' Blackstone said. 'Nobody ever caught a villain sitting in an office pushing a pen.'

The sergeant, whose name wasn't Green, dropped his pen, stood up and cast a melancholy glance over the pile of papers that would still be there when he got back. Following Blackstone from the room he caught up with the big man at pavement level and, although he knew the answer before he asked the question, ventured a small suggestion. 'Shall I get a car, sir?'

'You don't catch criminals from the back seat of a motor car,' he was told.

'No, sir,' the sergeant said, doing his best to keep pace with Blackstone who was striding along the pavement, his steel heel-plates sending an advance warning vibrating down the street. The sergeant had been with Blackstone for more than six months, which was some kind of record. Few of his predecessors had lasted more than half that time. For the life of him the sergeant couldn't work out what he was doing wrong. It certainly couldn't be that Blackstone was mellowing. He'd already bawled him out that week for coming to work without polishing his shoes and for loosening his tie when the temperature reached eighty in their small office.

'You're sure neither Reeder nor Toner has poked a nose out of doors for the last five or six weeks?'

'They've been out and about, sir.'

'You know what I mean. Neither of them has done anything unusual?'

'No, sir.'

'No shady meetings? No odd visitors, no breaks from routine?'

'No, sir.'

'How do they spend their evenings?'

'Toner sits at home with his wife and snotty kid watching the telly. Reeder plays poker at the Casino Royale twice a week. All usual stuff. The only night life either of them have had recently has been at the jazz club.'

The sergeant was six more paces along the pavement before he realized Detective-Chief Superintendent Blackstone wasn't alongside him. He turned and saw his superior officer staring at him, an expression of unconcealed disgust on his face. 'What jazz club?' Blackstone demanded in a quiet bellow.

'The South Bank Jazz Club in Monserrrat Road.'

'You didn't tell me about it, Green.'

The sergeant reduced the gap between them

to about three paces. 'Reeder's been a couple of times, maybe three. Toner was there last night.'

'Has either of them ever been there before?'

'No, sir.'

'Then why didn't you tell me?'

'Didn't think it mattered, sir. After all, they own it.'

'They own the curry shop and that poncing barber's shop but they don't go there.'

The sergeant decided against a reply, sensing that his unwitting error might have been a stroke of luck. Maybe, at long last, he had stumbled on the way to a transfer.

'What time does the club open?'

'About eight o'clock.'

Blackstone looked at his watch. 'Right, time for a pint and a pie then we'll have a look in. See what it is about the South Bank bleeding Jazz Club that interests our little Napoleon and his mate.'

He picked up his stride again and his sergeant fell into step beside him. 'It's very small-time. Bit tatty, if you ask me.'

'Jazz musicians are all either alcoholics or drug addicts,' Blackstone stated with great certainty. 'They're also layabouts and deadbeats.'

'Yes, sir,' the sergeant said in an attempt at agreement. He didn't know whether Blackstone was right or wrong. His own musical tastes ran to Johnny Cash and Marty Robbins – jazz was

41

unknown territory. He had no idea about Blackstone's musical likes and dislikes but hazarded a guess that if the Super liked anything it was probably Vera Lynn or a military band. Together, if such a thing was possible.

They reached the corner of Malbrook Road where the big man turned into the doors of the Golden Ball. With a sigh, his sergeant followed. Pies and pints with Blackstone were usually a fairly daunting prospect, not enough of the former and quite a few too many of the latter. Not that Detective-Chief Superintendent George Blackstone was a boozer, he just belonged to that generation of coppers who had served a lengthy part of their apprenticeship propping up bars in pubs, clubs and similar etablishments. In such places the imbibing of liquor could be comfortably blended with the assimilation of street-level information. The trouble was, such habits could lead to ulcers and hangovers in men like the sergeant, whose training had followed more academic patterns. He thought about his inadvertent error in neglecting to tell Blackstone about Reeder, Toner and the South Bank Jazz Club. He would have to play on that, he decided. With a bit of luck he might find himself on the move before too much longer. The thought of staying with the Super until his retirement in eleven months' time was more than flesh, blood and incipient ulcer could stand.

CHAPTER FIVE

Sid Toner stood on the pavement gradually clearing smoke from his lungs. He brushed fastidiously at his clothing in the hope that the smell of smoke would go away. Toner was in his late forties and he cultivated a manner, and helped rule a manor, to neither of which he'd been born. Always immaculate, he was dressed now in a mohair and cashmere mixture light grey suit; paler grey silk shirt with darker grey tie; grey socks and grey suede shoes. All of which, when added to his smoothly brushed prematurely grey hair and pale grey eyes, gave him a curiously flat appearance, a bit like a painting by numbers kit before all the colours had been filled in.

He thought back to the conversation he'd just had in the smoke-filled room. To some extent he was satisfied all was going well and he knew Reeder would approve. In fact Reeder, who believed the entire scheme was a product of Toner's brain, would be delighted. Needless to say, Toner wouldn't crack on that the plan was the product of another man's mind. Nothing would be gained by letting Reeder know that the Big Brain of South London's underworld didn't reside behind Toner's flat grey eyes but lurked instead behind eyes of a different colour which lived in a face Reeder knew but wouldn't suspect in a million years.

Toner opened the door of his wife's anonymous Mini, started the engine and eased away from the kerb. His mind went back to his recent conversation. There was one part of the proceedings which hadn't pleased him. The big Geordie with the tattooed ear lobes had an alarmingly casual attitude towards the impressively large quantity of miscellaneous explosives which filled one corner of the room. The explosives, allied to the fact that one of the Geordie's colleagues, a thin-faced dyspeptic Mancunian, was a chain smoker, had made him uneasy. All things considered, he was glad to be on his way home to Wimbledon and safety.

CHAPTER SIX

For a Thursday night, things were going very well. The club was more than three-quarters full, the bar staff were at full crack and curry was being eaten as fast as it could be slopped out.

Lew Jackson leaned his back against the bar and smiled amiably into the smoke-filled darkness of the room, mentally clocking up the takings. He felt a tug at his sleeve and turned to see Joe Nealis reaching over the bar.

44

'Harry's arrived and, God be praised, he's sober.'

'What kept him?'

'Car broke down.'

'Again?'

'Must be true, he'd be pissed out of his mind if it wasn't.'

'I expect you're right.' Lew glanced at his watch. 'Right, it's getting late. Got yourself organized?'

'Yes.'

'Okay, I'll prepare the big introduction.' Lew pushed himself upright, wandered through the tables lining the edge of the bar area and crossed the floor towards the miniature bandstand. He exchanged greetings with one or two of the club's regulars, avoiding the reproachful eyes of the Honeydripper who was plying her trade with a fat, bald, exceedingly drunk used car dealer from Vauxhall who seemed to have wandered into the club in the mistaken belief that he was entering a strip-joint. Honey seemed to be doing her best to convince him he was right in his assumption. She was wearing a long skirt, split up the front to show the colour of her knickers, and a blouse opened so far down the front it very nearly met the split in her skirt.

Lew made a mental note to make an effort to let her sing a couple of songs before the following week was out. The trouble was at that moment he was having difficulty in stopping the top of his head from falling off. In the time which had elapsed since his meeting with Eddie Lester he had wheeled, dealed, connived, pleaded, begged, cajoled and on two occasions even threatened, people until he didn't know whether he was reamed, bored or tapped. So far he had telephoned or visited at least twenty-five printers, none of whom seemed interested in producing his tickets, posters and programmes, at least not before Christmas. He had called every booking agency handling jazz musicians – not that there were very many of those around – and got equally nowhere, at least not with musicians of the calibre he wanted to hire. Even the local caterers appeared singularly unimpressed at the prospect of providing sausage rolls and cheese sandwiches for hordes of hopefully ravenous jazz fans. In fact the only bright spot in his efforts had been the venue. The official he'd spoken to about hiring the Town Hall had agreed without a moment's hesitation and had promised maximum co-operation. All things considered, he was finding the life of an impresario somewhat less attractive than he'd expected. The previous day he'd even thought about telephoning Jim Godbolt, who had managed his band back in the fifties, with a request for help but had decided against it. His relationship with Jim, whose tongue had been every bit as sharp as his own, had been marked by the time-honoured friction which always exists between artiste and agent. With that in mind there was no reason to suppose the Bolt from God, who was now engaged in a new career as an author, would be very interested in helping out an old adversary.

Closer to home, Joe Nealis hadn't been all that helpful. With some justification he had pointed out that if he was expected to do his own and Lew's work at the club he couldn't very well spare any time to organize a jazz festival.

Lew reached the stage and cocked an ear at the tape playing behind the buzz of conversation, identified it and, as it stopped, nodded at Oscar, the barman, who switched off the tape recorder.

'Evening one and all,' Lew said into one of the microphones, and paused until more than half the punters stopped talking to listen to him. 'Sorry you've had to listen to more recorded than live jazz tonight but our star guest's transport broke down. To be precise he lost the chain off his bike down Munster Road and a Fulham supporter pinched it to keep his trousers up. Now, if you didn't already know, you've just been listening to a tape by Art Blakey. From one drummer to another and in this case from the sublime to the ridiculous, give a welcome please to our resident band leader, Joe Nealis.' He stepped back and led a ripple of disinterested applause for Joe who gangled on to the stage, bobbed his head, sat down and gave

47

himself an encouraging little roll on his snare drum. Lew continued, 'On bass tonight we have Curley Shatner. Some of you look old enough to remember Curly from the days of the Tubby Hayes big band.' He paused for even less applause. 'And on piano, Sammy Allon.' This time the applause was a little more enthusiastic. Allon had played around the London area for almost as long as anyone could remember. He was the dependable type, always turned up on time, could be relied upon to make an inferior musician sound good and a good one sound better. Lew couldn't hire him as often as he would have liked, which was a pity because most of the musicians he was obliged to hire needed someone like Sammy behind them. 'Okay,' Lew went on after Sammy had acknowledged the applause and had sat down. 'Now an equally warm welcome please for an old friend of ours and yours, the one and only Harry Betts.' He stepped down from the stage and clapped his hands vigorously as he headed back towards the bar.

Behind him he heard Joe count the group in on a medium-bounce tempo and they swung easily into the opening bars of *Sweet Georgia Brown*. Reaching the bar, he picked up the glass he'd left there, swallowed the remains of its contents and pushed it across to Oscar who refilled it without being asked.

'Hello, Lew.'

48

Lew turned to see the Honeydripper, who had left her target for the night and was sitting on one of the bar stools, looking dejected. 'Hi, Honey,' he said. He took a deep breath. 'Listen, remember what I said about you singing a song or two for me? Stay behind tonight, after we close. We'll run through one or two numbers and if it sounds like working, I'll fit you in for a couple of small spots next week.'

The Honeydripper beamed widely, all her dejection gone in a flash. She threw a long, thin arm around his neck and kissed him wetly. 'Oh, Lew, thanks, thanks a lot.'

'Hey, what the fuck's going on?' a slurred voice said, and the used car dealer from Vauxhall lurched in between them.

'Okay, sweetheart,' Honey said. 'Just saying hello to a friend of mine.'

'Oh yeah? Well, so long as I'm paying for the fucking drinks you keep your fucking hands off him.'

'Watch your language and keep your voice down,' Lew said in a fairly friendly manner.

'Who the fucking hell do you think you're talking to?' the fat man said, grabbing one of Lew's lapels with one hand, the other gripping the edge of the bar in case he fell over.

Lew felt his stomach squirm. He didn't like violence, had even been known to run from it, but very occasionally had to face up to it in the line of duty. Fortunately there were few

49

occasions when trouble flared up in the club. Jazz fans were, on the whole, a fairly peaceable bunch but there was always the odd-ball who broke the pattern. In this case the man wasn't a fan, didn't belong and was very obviously about to step out of line.

'I own this club,' he said equably, hoping his voice sounded steadier than he felt. 'If you can't behave yourself I shall have to ask you to leave.'

'You and whose fucking army?'

'How about mine?' another voice interrupted.

The fat man and Lew looked, with equal surprise, at the interrupter. Lew didn't recognize the big man but the used car dealer did. 'Sorry, Mr Blackstone,' he said. Dropping his grip on Lew's lapel he scuttled for the stairs as if his trousers were on fire.

'Thanks,' Lew said, trying to sound as if he could have coped alone. On the stand, Harry Betts had moved into a slow, liquid interpretation of *'Tis Autumn* sounding quite unlike the pale imitation of Stan Getz most tenor players did when they tried that particular tune.

'That sort of riff-raff regular here?' the big man asked.

'No.'

'Oh. Prefer people like Jack Reeder and Sid Toner, do you?'

Lew stared at the man. 'What's that supposed to mean?'

'Toner was here last night. Reeder's been

here several times recently. Friends of yours, are they?'

'They're my landlords, if it's anything to do with you.'

'Everything has something to do with me.'

'You don't look like Jesus Christ,' Lew said.

'Blasphemer as well are you, Jackson? My word but you won't go to heaven, will you?'

'Conversations like this will be the death of television,' Lew said.

'Is that supposed to be a joke? You'll have to tell me if it is because I haven't got a sense of humour. That is something several villains will be happy to confirm. Quite a few have tried little jokes on me. They usually ended up inside with plenty of time to laugh at their own jokes. Mind you, none of them stayed inside as long as they should. There's always some bleeding-heart ready to stick his nose in.'

'Ah,' Lew said. 'Policeman, are you?'

'There's a clever lad.'

Lew sensed, rather than saw, the Honeydripper begin to edge away. 'I like to think so,' he said.

'So, all the lovey-dovey between you and the Reeder–Toner bunch is just landlord and tenant, is it? Well, keep it that way, Jackson, then you and me won't have any cause to test my lack of humour.' On the bandstand Harry Betts finished *'Tis Autumn* and without waiting for the applause to die down snapped his fingers for Joe

51

to kick off into an up-tempo treatment of *Outer Drive*. 'That's something else, I don't like,' the policeman said into Lew's ear, one finger pointing at the four musicians. 'I don't like any kind of music and least of all jazz, rock and roll and similar shit. I'd close places like this down and have people like that locked up where they couldn't do any harm to ordinary, decent people.'

'Is that right?' Lew said cheerfully.

'Oh, yes, that's right, Jackson. Remember that and we might avoid any future difficulties.'

'Good of you to take the trouble to tell me.'

'Isn't it though.' The big policeman moved away, went up the stairs and out of the club, leaving Lew feeling unaccountably disturbed and completely unaware that a thin-faced, miserable-looking man who had come in with Blackstone was still there, further down the bar, one hand wrapped round a glass of neat tomato juice, the other massaging his stomach.

Lew thought about having another drink but decided against it. He would try to get an early night. Tomorrow would have to be another hard slog around the agencies. If he didn't get things together soon he would be well and truly in the mire. Apart from that it seemed positively indecent not to be taking advantage of all the money from which Eddie Lester was so eager to be parted.

The musicians were still working on *Outer*

Drive and he listened more attentively to Harry Betts. He really was sounding good. Maybe he should talk to him about the festival. Fairly low on the bill though.

When Harry Betts finished his set Lew wandered over to the stage, applauding enough to keep the audience going but not so much that Harry would ask for a rise.

'Okay,' he told the punters. 'Harry will be back later. Until then it's time I raised the level of the entertainment up to its usual mediocrity.' He sat down at the piano recently vacated by Sammy Allon and began a slow-tempo version of Billy Strayhorn's *'A' Train*. After the first chorus he put in the familiar Duke Ellington intro and knocked out the rest of the number at its more familiar pace.

He sang two more songs, *Lady Be Good* and *Corinne, Corinne*, the last one getting the audience stamping away, more or less on the beat. Being a great believer in quitting while he was in front, he reintroduced Harry Betts and left the stage.

He looked around for the Honeydripper but she hadn't reappeared after going into hiding from Blackstone. Lew headed for the stairs. Joe could lock up, he decided. After all, he usually did.

As he opened the door to the street he saw the Honeydripper hovering uncertainly in a doorway a few yards away.

'Going already, Lew?' she asked.

'Hard day today, even harder tomorrow,' he said.

'You said we might try some songs.'

'Oh, Christ. Sorry, Honey, I forgot. All the excitement with your fat friend and the large arm of the law.' To prove he had no plans for going back to the club Lew started walking and, after a moment's hesitation, Honey fell in step beside him. She seemed taller than usual and, glancing down, he saw she was teetering along on extra-high heels. He felt mildly relieved that, in addition to all his other troubles, he hadn't started shrinking.

'Sorry about Gus,' she said.

'Gus? That's fatso's name, is it?'

'Yes. I didn't bring him in, he was there when I arrived. And he was drunk to start with.'

'No sweat, the redoubtable Mr Blackstone seemed to put the fear of God into him without even trying. You too, if it comes to that.'

They had reached the corner of Oxford Road when Lew hesitated. The Honeydripper seemed to know why before he did. 'Broke again, Lew?'

'I usually am by this time of day.'

'We can have this one on credit.'

'That'll make two on the trot.'

'The last one wasn't on credit, it was on the house.'

'Bad for business, doing things like that, Honey.'

'It's my business.'

'Still managing to stay freelance?'

'Yes. I wouldn't do it if I had to work for Mr Reeder or one of the other organizers.'

'Spoken like a true believer in private enterprise. Right—your place or mine?'

She turned up her nose. 'Mine, yours isn't very cheerful.'

'Gee, thanks,' Lew said, trying not to feel affronted.

The Honeydripper's business premises were in Disraeli Road and consisted of a single, large room decorated principally in red. By day the effect was garish but at night with only subdued lighting it was warm, friendly and sexy. The furnishings were all good and included a wide, comfortable bed, a divan against one wall, a thick white sheepskin rug in front of a log-effect electric fire and heavy curtains which, when drawn, easily turned day into night. A curtained-off alcove had once been a small kitchen but now boasted a toilet, a bidet and a wash-basin, all much more suitable for the needs of Honey and her clients.

Lew dropped heavily on to the divan, took off his shoes and yawned hugely.

'Tired?' the Honeydripper asked as she sat on the bed.

'Must be my age.'

His yawn was contagious and the girl followed suit, stretching her arms high above her head as she did so, the action causing her open-fronted blouse to open still further. Lew stood up, crossed to the bed, leaned down and kissed her between the breasts.

'Just a second, Lew.' She stood up and took off her blouse and split skirt which left her dressed only in a pair of tiny red knickers and knee-high boots. 'The clothes are new,' she explained.

Lew didn't answer but reached out for her. Fifteen minutes later, still wearing his shirt, tie and socks, he was fast asleep, snoring loudly. The girl disengaged herself gently and stood up to unzip and remove her boots before lying down again beside him. The Honeydripper snuggled up to him, her head resting on his chest, but she didn't sleep. Instead she lay, eyes open and slightly wet with what could have been tears, thinking about herself and her life in terms which would have surprised Lew had she voiced them. It would have surprised him even more had he known how much he featured in those thoughts and for what reasons.

Lew woke some hours later, switched on the bedside light and peered at his watch. It was almost five o'clock and he lay there trying to control his natural bodily functions by sheer willpower. He failed and slid out of the bed and padded behind the curtain into the alcove. Back in bed again a few moments later he looked at the girl, fast asleep beside him. He felt mildly

56

guilty at the fact that he used her as casually as he did but then shrugged the thought away. After all, her life was built around casual sex.

He tried to remember when he'd had any sexual experience which wasn't casual and failed. He supposed the relationships he'd had with his wives during the first weeks of his two marriages had been more than that but he couldn't honestly remember. He didn't think about that side of his life too often but when he did it depressed him. He was inclined to shrug it off as part of the life of a professional musician but it didn't work. At bottom he knew it was him, not his profession, which was at fault.

Throughout his career he had carefully cultivated an on-stage image of larger-than-life bonhomie. When the band had been on the road they'd followed the tradition of the era – some had worn straw boaters and floral silk waistcoats, others bowler hats, some bands wore blazers and flannels which made them look like slightly dissipated cricket teams. Lew Jackson's Southern Syncopaters had worn bookmaker check suits, two-tone shoes and, as leader, singer, MC and occasional comic relief, Lew had added a smart line in Oscar-Wildean floppy velvet hats. His manner suited his flamboyant appearance – casual, off-hand, a joke for every occasion, even if most of his had been pinched from other people. He wasn't quite certain at what point the on-stage persona had become

57

part of the off-stage man, but it had happened.

By the time the band had folded he was wearing the suits and hats all the time and the jokes were there all the time too. Without them he felt too exposed, too vulnerable to the vicissitudes of normal, everyday life, a life he neither understood nor wanted.

He yawned and looked at his watch again. It wasn't much past five and he didn't feel like sleep. He touched Honey's shoulder but then changed his mind, turned away and switched off the light. He dozed fitfully for the next hour or so before getting up and dressing.

He went back to his own flat, made coffee and toasted the remains of a sliced loaf which was beginning to look slightly suspect. He spent a couple of minutes making up a shopping list of groceries to give to Oscar, the barman, who also bought the makings for the club's kitchen. The thought crossed his mind that there were some things for which he missed having a permanent relationship with a woman. Then he grinned wryly, realizing that most of the women he knew would apply a very sharp knee in the groin at such evidence of male supremacy thinking.

After abandoning the remains of the toast to a pedal-bin which needed emptying, he swallowed the dregs of the coffee and put his mind on to the more practical matters of the festival. Unfortunately there was nothing about the festival that made him feel particularly cheerful. He decided he was becoming extremely negative in his thinking, about the festival and about his lifestyle. It wasn't like him, not like him at all. Now wasn't the time to start taking anything too seriously—there would be time for that when he was dead.

CHAPTER SEVEN

The telephone was ringing when Lew unlocked the door later that morning. He hurried down the stairs, working on the principle that the way things had been recently there wasn't much chance the call could bring news that would make matters worse than they were. The telephone was in the tiny office jammed between the bar and the entrance to the tiny kitchen. For a moment he didn't recognize the caller's voice, then it registered. It was one of the booking agencies he'd talked to several times in the past few days. He felt a sudden glow of hope.

'About your festival,' the voice said.

'Yes?'

'We've had a cancellation at the Pizza Express. They're having some problems and are having to close over August Bank Holiday. The guys they'd booked will be free.'

'Who are they?'

'Kenny Davern and Dave McKenna. Any use

to you?'

Lew swallowed and tried to sound casual. 'They'll do fine. What's the rate?'

The voice stated a figure which made Lew feel dizzy, but he remembered the ten thousand up front being provided by Eddie Lester and agreed the deal before he got cold feet.

After replacing the telephone he stared at the wall trying not to get too excited. With Davern and McKenna he at last had something with which to bang the drum. With men of their calibre he would soon be taken much more seriously. He clapped his hands together and went out of the office, to be met by Joe Nealis.

'You're in early.'

'So are you. What's the matter? Wet the bed again?'

'Tut, tut. Sorry I split early last night, mate. Felt the need of some sleep.'

'It's your age.'

'Harry was playing well last night. You all were in fact, but Harry was something of a revelation.'

Joe nodded. 'Best Betts I've ever heard.'

'I thought I was the one who did the jokes.'

'That was a joke?'

Lew grinned at his partner, who was clearly in a much more cheerful frame of mind than usual. He decided to raise the matter of the Harry Betts Quartet's appearance at the festival. 'How would you like to appear on the same bill as Kenny Davern?' he asked.

'*The* Kenny Davern?'

'You mean there's more than one of him?'

'You're not telling me you've got him for your half-assed festival?'

'Oh yes I have. And Dave McKenna.'

'Well, bloody hell. No wonder you're looking pleased with yourself.'

'Yeah, well, what I thought was, seeing old Harry's found a new lease of life, what about keeping the four of you together as one of the supporting bands?'

Joe nodded, his enthusiasm making itself apparent in a fusillade of blinking eyelids. 'Sure, why not?'

Lew nodded. 'Why not. You on?'

'Sure, I'll talk to Harry if you like. Might have to offer him a sweetener if he has to stay sober.'

'Could give him billing,' Lew said, trying to keep it casual.

'Fine with me.'

Lew grinned, pleased to have overcome one hurdle. 'Great,' he said.

'There's not a lot of time left,' Joe remarked. Lew nodded, relieved that Joe appeared to have reconciled himself to the fact that the festival was a very short time away. 'I suppose you're going to need some help after all,' Nealis went on.

'Thanks, mate.'

Nealis frowned. 'Wait a minute. I thought Davern and McKenna were booked into the Pizza Express over August Bank Holiday.'

'They've cancelled.'

'Oh, that accounts for it then. Funnily enough I was talking about them to Sid Toner.'

'Sid Toner?'

'Yes. I told you he was in here night before last.'

'So?'

'He was interested in how you were getting on with your festival bookings. I told him you weren't. Then he asked who was on where and when. I went through this month's *Jazz Journal* with him, telling him who everyone was. He seemed particularly interested in Davern and McKenna. Don't ask me why.'

'Maybe he's seen the light.'

'Could be. Anyway, he was very matey. Even offered his services should we ever need to call on him.'

'Services for what?'

'He didn't specify. Here, he left his card.' Nealis handed a visiting card to Lew, who glanced at it and added it to a clutter of papers and odds and ends bulging from a wallet filled with everything except money. For a moment he thought about the sudden interest in their welfare and music being shown by their landlord and the local police. It occurred to him that he should mention to Joe the visit of the big policeman. Then he decided against it—Joe was a born worrier. It would be better to keep quiet about it, especially now Joe was offering to help him with the festival.

'Right, what do we do first?' Joe asked.

'Try all the agencies again, this time telling them who we've got booked already. Might make a difference.'

Joe nodded and had turned towards the office door when the telephone rang again. He reached for the instrument and answered it. When he replaced it he gave Lew a beaming smile and a thumb's-up sign. 'Now you're really on your way.'

'Why?'

'You've got Ray Curtis and the Chicago Big Band.'

'Christ. How come?'

'They were booked into the Fiesta Club in Stockton over the Bank Holiday.'

'So?'

'So they've had a fire at the club and won't be able to get it fixed in time.'

'Great. Not about the club but. . . .'

'Yes, I know. It's an ill wind.'

'Have you ever met him?'

'Curtis? No, I haven't.'

'He has quite a reputation.'

'He plays bloody fine alto and the band's always good.'

'He's been known to punch people he doesn't

63

like.'

'So what. He'll love us. Top billing at a London festival when he might have been making an early return to the States.'

Lew nodded. 'Like you said, it's an ill wind. Let's hope it blows Mr Curtis an improvement in his temper.'

'The way your luck seems to have changed he'll probably turn out to have signed the pledge and be all sweetness and light.'

'Maybe,' Lew said. He glanced at his watch. 'Anyway, what are you doing here at this time?'

'I could ask you the same question.'

'I've got work to do.'

Nealis looked away and shrugged. 'It's somewhere to come,' he said. 'An empty flat doesn't have a lot to offer. You're used to it, I'm not.'

'Empty flat? Where's Chris?' Chris was Joe's wife, a fiercely independent woman with very positive views on just about everything and everyone, including Lew Jackson. Her views on him were sharp, rather bitter and had resulted in more than one difficult patch with his partner.

'Chris and I have had a few differences,' Nealis said.

'What does that mean?'

'It means she's gone home to mother, in a manner of speaking.'

'Oh, bloody hell. I'm sorry, mate. when did

this happen?'

Nealis grinned, without humour. 'About six months ago.'

'Six . . . are you kidding me?'

'No, like you keep telling me, I leave the jokes to you.'

'But why in God's name didn't you say something before now?'

'I could say you never asked, but to be honest I didn't think anything would be gained by talking about it.'

Lew didn't answer. He had known Joe for thirty years. They had played together on one night stands up and down the country. They had got drunk together. They had even, on one whisky-soaked night in Liverpool, taken turns with the same band-following scrubber. They had run up debts together. They had shared the lease of the club for longer than the lifetime of some of their members. But none of that seemed to have done anything to bring them particularly close together as people. He became aware that Joe was watching him with an expression of mild amusement on his face. He raised an enquiring eyebrow.

'I was just thinking, people are funny,' Joe said.

'Meaning?'

'Meaning, we seem to have stuck together longer than the average marriage these days. Maybe it's something to do with the fact that we don't talk very much.'

'We talk.'

'But not about the things some people seem to think matter.'

Lew headed for the bar and picked up the whisky bottle and a glass. 'I don't think I can stand a philosophical discussion at this time of the day without some moral support.' He turned back to Joe, the bottle in his hand. 'Look, I know I'm no expert, I've tried being married twice and come unstuck at the seams both times, but if there's anything I can do, even if it's just to stand here and be talked at, then feel free.'

Nealis nodded his head. 'Thanks. Let's forget it for now, but if the need arises I'll holler.'

Lew looked at the bottle and shook his head. 'Well, if there's to be no philosophical discussion then there's no excuse for this either.'

'Right,' Nealis said. 'Let's make a start. Who do I call?'

Lew passed him a list of names and numbers and Joe picked up the telephone and began to dial. Lew stood in the office door, watching but not really listening. His mind had eagerly moved away from involvement with his partner's personal problems, not out of lack of concern but through simple unwillingness to get involved in areas which he knew from experience were completely unsolvable. He turned his mind instead to the sudden surge of coincidental cancellations. Well, maybe two cancellations were not a surge but they were enough to cause a raised eyebrow. Now didn't seem a good time to start questioning his luck but he decided it wouldn't do any harm to stay alert. It was a good resolution, and like all similar resolutions he had made over the years he very soon forgot all about it.

CHAPTER EIGHT

'Any problems?'

'Nothing I can't handle.'

'What does that mean?'

'We had a slow start but that's been overcome. Everything else will fall into place. If it doesn't, we give it a helpful nudge.'

'You won't show your hand?'

Sid Toner laughed softly. 'Of course not.'

'Good.' The other man leaned back against the leather upholstery of the Rolls-Royce. 'When are you going to make your move?'

Faintly, in the far distance, a fire-engine bell shrilled. 'Soon,' Toner said.

'Eddie Lester won't give you any trouble?'

'That crud? He owes us too much. He didn't make his fortune with nothing more than what he keeps between his ears, even if he and the papers like to think so. He borrowed heavily in the early days and from time to time he's needed a few competitors frightening off. We helped with both problems and a few others.' He grinned tightly, thinking about the difficulty in finding singing whores.

'As long as you're happy,' his companion said. 'Very well, I'll telephone you in about a week. Then you won't hear from me until it's all over.'

'Where are you going . . . for your holidays?'

The hesitation wasn't lost on the other man but he didn't mind Toner's little dig. Toner was, after all, taking a risk. Not a big one but a risk all the same. 'Vienna,' he told him.

'Nice place,' Sid said, remembering seeing *The Third Man* on the telly a couple of years back. He opened the car door, climbed out, then turned and leaned back in to shake hands. 'Be seeing you,' he said. A car passed, briefly illuminating Toner and the open door of the Rolls.

The other man pulled back into the shadow of the car. 'Best of luck,' he said.

When Toner's wife's Mini and the dark blue Rolls-Royce had disappeared from sight, a shadow in a doorway fifty yards away moved and grew legs. The figure walked stiffly along the street to a telephone kiosk, went inside and dialled a number.

Detective-Chief Superintendent George Blackstone listened to the sergeant's report and made a note of the registration number of the Rolls. Then he grunted and came near to making a compliment. 'Good man, Green,' he said. 'Get some shuteye and be here bright and early tomorrow.'

'Yes, sir,' the sergeant said and went home, hoping against hope that his wife wouldn't have fried something for his supper.

In his office Blackstone looked at the vehicle number he had scrawled on his blotter. He didn't bother to put it through the system—the number was burned into his mind and he knew that, try as he might, he wouldn't be able to nail anything on the man. Still, the information had its uses. He made a telephone call and set a few wheels in motion. By noon the following day he would know where the owner of the Rolls-Royce was going for his holiday, which didn't interest him, but, more important, he would know when he would be taking those holidays and that did interest him. It interested him very much indeed.

He sat there for another hour, thinking, motionless, his big hands resting on the desk ready to leap up and attack if the need arose. He was experiencing very mixed feelings. There was a suppressed excitement coming from the certain knowledge that things were building up. There was also frustration from the equally certain knowledge that he had nothing which would make sense to anyone else. It didn't even make sense to him. Just little oddments, unrelated snippets of information, impressions.

He picked up one of the Collator's pieces of paper. It had been lying around the office for a day or two and he still didn't know if it fitted anywhere in his puzzle. A sudden rush of unexplained damage to various properties up and down the country. Properties that had one thing in common, which was why the Collator had spotted the connection, if connection it was. He leaned on his desk and pushed himself upwards. It was time he talked to Lew Jackson again. He looked at his watch. That tatty club would be closed by now—tomorrow would have to do. He would have to go home instead.

The Chief Superintendent's face twisted in a spasm of gloom. Home was a large, lonely room on the first floor of an old house in Castello Avenue which he shared with a handful of pieces of ageing furniture and memories of a short-lived marriage which hadn't stood the strains of a policeman's life. The thought of retirement suddenly seemed a lot less attractive than usual. Spending his nights in the room was bad enough. Having to spend days there as well would be murder, absolute bloody murder.

CHAPTER NINE

'We've done it. We've gone and bloody well done it.' Lew did a couple of dance steps which were almost graceful, but spoiled the effect by crashing against one of the tables and sending it tumbling over, its tin ashtray rolling noisily across the floor towards the bandstand.

Joe Nealis grinned cheerfully, not a blink in sight. The three days of concerts were fully set up. Three big bands, six small groups, two solo piano players and two solo singers, not to mention promises from half a dozen London-based musicians to drop in as guests with one or another of the bands. Programmes, posters and tickets were being printed, the caterers were busily churning out several miles of sausage rolls to be put into the freezer until the day before they were required. Hotel accommodation was arranged and about three tons of miscellaneous lighting and sound equipment was hired, ready to be set up in the Town Hall.

'Fan-bloody-tastic,' Lew said, picking up the table and looking in vain for the ashtray.

'I must say I didn't expect to see the day.'

'Pessimist.'

'Never touched a drop, all day.'

'My God, jokes yet. Right,' Lew said. 'Let's get all those bits of paper into some sort of order

71

then I'll take a ride into darkest Hampstead to see our benefactor.'

Joe followed him into the office. 'What does it all add up to?' he asked.

'Advance booking fees, reservation charges, odd and sods. Three thousand. That leaves seven in hand. Mind you, most of that will go before we open.'

Joe picked up a hand-written draft of the entire festival's concerts. There were five in all. Saturday afternoon and evening, the same on Sunday and the final one on Monday afternoon. 'Never thought the day would dawn when I'd see my name on the same bill as Kenny Davern, Ray Curtis, Big Mama Richards, Art Blakey, Clark Terry and Scott Hamilton.'

'To say nothing of Joe Williams and Dizzy Gillespie.'

'Like you said, fan-bloody-tastic.'

'Yes, pity about Carrie Smith though. Now there's a singer. Still, a recording session is a recording session, and if she has to be in New York over August Bank Holiday there's nothing we can do about it.'

'Lucky we got Big Mama Richards at such short notice.'

'Right,' Lew turned, his hands full of folders, scraps of paper and other odds and ends. 'I'm on my way. I should be back by ten. I haven't felt so good in ages. Maybe give you guys the benefit of my tonsils tonight.'

'What have we done to deserve that?'

'Comedian, I'm the one who tells the jokes, remember.'

'Only when you manage to steal them from Ronnie Scott.'

'Speaking of whom, I just might wander in there tonight on my way back.'

'Why?'

'I feel like a gloat, that's why.'

'If you do that, you won't be back before the punters have to be torn away from their moorings.'

'Ah well, maybe I'll save the gloat for another day.' Lew manoeuvred his way past Nealis and headed for the stairs. 'I think I'll go round to Honey's place, take her with me,' he added.

'At your age screwing in a car can be dangerous. It uses muscles you haven't used before.'

'Who said anything about screwing? Just thought she might like to see her friend Lester again.'

'Liar.'

Lew made a rude noise as he reached the top of the stairs and elbowed the door open.

Behind him, in the club's tiny office, Joe Nealis was still sitting, staring at the poster draft. For a moment he allowed himself the unaccustomed luxury of a daydream. He hadn't expected Lew to get this far but now he had, maybe, just maybe, they might be back in the big time after twenty-odd years in the wilderness. Then he forced the thought away. Wait until it was all over and the dust had settled. Then would be the time to count the benefits, not now.

As Lew drove away from the club his thoughts were in no way as cautious as his partner's. He had no doubts, no doubts at all about the future. He was on his way to the place he deserved. The top.

His high good humour wasn't disturbed by the absence of the Honeydripper from the house she shared with her family and from the tiny flat in Disraeli Road. She must have made an early start, he guessed. He sang cheerfully most of the way up to Hampstead. He didn't stop singing until he reached Eddie Lester's front door. There he stopped and for quite some time doubted very much if he would ever feel like singing again.

'What do you mean, gone?' he demanded.

The grey-haired little man in a boiler suit who had opened Lester's front door shrugged his shoulders. 'Gone means gone, dunnit. Gone, gone, gone.'

'Where to?'

'Abroad.'

'What about his wife and kids?'

'They've gone with him. The dogs are in kennels and the bleeding hamster's at his mother's.'

'William.'

'What?'

'The hamster, William.'

'No, William's dead. Little bleeder. This one's called Ernest. Bleeding silly name for a hamster if you ask me.'

'For Christ's sake stop talking about bloody hamsters,' Lew yelled. 'Where's he gone?' He thought hard. 'Portugal. He has a villa there.'

'No, not Portugal.'

'Where then?'

'Why should I tell you?'

'Because I have to....' Lew broke off, fumbled in his pocket, scattering papers around him as he did so. He thrust a pound note at the little man in the boiler suit. 'Where has he gone?'

'Hong Kong.'

Lew stared at him in silence. After a long, long time he realized he was holding his breath. He let it out slowly and carefully. 'Hong Kong,' he repeated.

'Hong Kong,' the little man agreed.

'How long for?'

'Two months.'

Lew turned away and managed to open the Granada's door. He threw the papers on the front seat, then picked up those he'd dropped and added them to the pile. After he had climbed into the car himself he started the engine and managed to drive about two miles

75

before his brain began to function. When it did he pulled into the kerbside, turned off the ignition, rested his head on the steering-wheel and tried to make up his mind whether to cry, scream or merely close his eyes and drive down Finchley Road until he hit a number 13 bus.

In the house on East Heath Road the little man in the boilersuit was dialling a number on an imitation antique French telephone which stood on the bar in the white-carpeted living-room 'He's been and gone, Mr Toner,' he said when his call was answered.

'No problems?'

'None.'

'Okay, Herbie. Lock up and come back here.'

'Yes, Mr Toner.'

'And Herbie.'

'Yes, Mr Toner?'

'Only one drink, Herbie.'

'Yes, Mr Toner.' The little man replaced the telephone and poured himself a scotch, not a small one, a tumblerful. If Mr Toner said one drink, then one drink it was.

Along Finchley Road Lew Jackson straightened up and stared blankly out of the windscreen. He didn't know the whats, the whys and the wherefores, but he knew a mess when he saw one. He thought hard about going back to see Joe but ruled that out. A volley of 'I told you so's' wouldn't solve anything. He fumbled among the papers on the seat beside

76

him. The contract he'd signed with Eddie
Lester was there, so switching on the overhead
light and screwing up his eyes he read it. When
he'd finished he let it drop from his fingers
wondering why he hadn't read it as carefully
before he signed it. He knew the answer to that
one. Greed. Ambition. And plain old-fashioned
stupidity.

He was halfway along Old Brompton Road
before he thought of something that might, just
might, get him out of the mess he was in.
Fumbling in his wallet with one hand he came
up with Sid Toner's card. He stopped at a
telephone kiosk and dialled the first of the two
numbers there. Two minutes later he was in the
car again, heading for Wimbledon. He felt a tiny
bit more cheerful. It never occurred to him that
he was also being just as greedy as before, just as
ambitious. And just as plain, old-fashioned,
bloody stupid.

CHAPTER TEN

'What do you mean, a change of backer?'

Lew rested one hand on the bar, the other
tightening its grip on a glass containing a liberal
dose of Scottish reviving fluid. 'I mean,
someone else is putting up the money, in place
of Eddie Lester.'

'Who?'

Lew took a long drink and closed his eyes. 'Jack Reeder,' he said. Several moments of painful silence passed and eventually he opened his eyes to see what had happened to Joe Nealis.

His partner hadn't passed out with shock, wasn't glowing bright red with rage, wasn't even blinking furiously. Instead, he was staring across the floor towards the deserted bandstand. After a long, long time he sighed and nodded his head slowly. 'I knew it was all too good to be true,' he said quietly. 'There had to be a catch somewhere and this is it.'

For a moment Lew didn't answer. There wasn't all that much to say. He took another drink and looked at his reflection in the mirror behind the bar. The face looking back at him was bleak and miserable, and even the suit appeared somewhat subdued.

He sighed. 'Reeder's money is as good as Lester's. Okay, maybe its origins leave something to be desired, but it's still spendable scratch.'

Joe turned to face him and shook his head. 'You don't believe that any more than I do. If Reeder's putting up cash like that, there has to be something in it for him.'

'Such as?'

'I don't know, maybe he wants your skin on his lampshade.'

'He's offering very nearly the same deal as

Lester.'

'Very nearly?'

'He takes a higher percentage of the profits.'

'How much higher?'

'Half as much again.'

'Is that all?' Nealis remarked.

His partner appeared not to notice the sarcasm. 'We'll have to make our own arrangements for recording the concerts. Reeder doesn't want any part in that. Everything we make out of the recordings is ours.'

'Ours?'

'We're still partners, aren't we?'

Nealis looked at Lew carefully. 'Christ Almighty,' he said. 'I do believe on Judgment Day you'll be up there offering autographed copies of your latest record.'

'That's better, mate. Nothing's ever as black as it looks.'

'You'd better tell me everything that's happened. Starting with our former benefactor. Why is he no longer behind us?'

Briefly, inevitably so because there wasn't much to tell, Lew told Nealis about Lester's sudden, unexplained departure for the Far East. When he got to the part about the small print on the contract he had signed with Lester, which made him entirely responsible for all contracts signed in the name of the promoters, Joe's eyes began to blink rapidly. In the circumstances Lew decided it was a good sign. At any rate it was better than the stony impassivity with which his original revelation had been greeted. When he described his visit to Sid Toner's Wimbledon home and the subsequent meeting with Jack Reeder, Nealis's blinking reached a new high. 'What have you signed this time?' he asked.

'Nothing.'

'Nothing?'

'We're doing it on trust.'

'Trust?'

'I trust them to fit me up with a pair of concrete slippers if I try any fancy stuff.'

'What if they pull out, like Lester did?'

'Unlikely. They wouldn't want in if they didn't have. . . .' Lew's voice trailed away.

Nealis snapped up the unfinished sentence. 'So, you think they have reasons for what they're doing?'

'Of course they have reasons. They can see a profit,' Lew said, aware of the lack of conviction in his tone.

'I don't like it,' Joe said.

Lew didn't answer, because the truth was he didn't like it very much himself, but he needed cash and he needed it quickly. While he would have run a mile from borrowing from people like Reeder and Toner in normal circumstances, these were not normal. He was stuck with a fully booked series of concerts, and if he dropped everything at this stage he would be in hock for at least three thousand pounds. Maybe a few thousand more if some of the people involved decided to sue. The prospect of legal action didn't alarm him. He didn't have the money and blood couldn't be extracted from stone as he had proved over and over again to the men from the Inland Revenue. The trouble with such action was that he would have to close the club, leaving him with no income of any kind, and worse, he would lose any remaining vestige of credibility in the profession, to say nothing of losing for ever any chance of being able to stage a two-bit concert, let alone a three-day festival.

He looked at his watch. It was almost four o'clock in the morning but any need for sleep had been passed by. He frowned suddenly. 'What are you doing here at this time anyway?' he asked.

'Like I told you the other day, an empty flat doesn't hold a lot of joy.'

'Try filling it with some, mate.'

'Like what, for instance?'

'Like the Honeydripper, for instance.'

'Take her in permanently, you mean?'

'Why not? She's a good fuck and she doesn't get in the way.'

'You must be joking.'

'Well, maybe not permanently. Just until you get over the hump. Or the humping.'

'I don't think so. Anyway, she spends most of her time talking about you.'

'Me?'

'Seems to be worried about you, either that or she fancies you.'

'You're joking.'

'Ask her yourself.'

'I'm not sure I'm interested.'

Joe shrugged. 'Suit yourself, it's just that the last couple of days or so she's been a bit depressed.'

'Oh, that. Probably my fault, I offered her a singing job and I haven't delivered.'

'Maybe that's it then. Seriously though, if she wasn't a hooker, she'd be a nice girl.'

'What've you got against hookers?' Lew said, grinning.

Nealis shrugged. 'Okay, get the joke book out.'

Lew finished his drink in one swallow. 'Well, whatever the delights of lonely flats, I reckon it's time for bed for me.'

'I'll lock up,' Joe said.

'You usually do.'

'True. Listen, Lew. You have told me everything, this time, haven't you? No little secrets you're saving until a better moment? The way things are, this is probably the best moment there's going to be.'

Lew shook his head. 'Nothing, only. . . .'

'Only?'

'Only Reeder has offered to supply all the help we'll need at the festival. Ticket collectors, bar staff, stage-hands, bouncers—not that we should need any of those.'

'Why?'

'Why?'

'What's in it for him?'

'That way he can keep an eye on all the action, I expect.'

Nealis shook his head slowly. 'Well, there's an old saying about looking gift horses in the mouth, so maybe I'd better keep quiet, but. . . .' He turned away without letting Lew ask what the doubt in his mind was. Not that Lew needed to do anything of the sort. He knew what was worrying Nealis because it was worrying him too. Reeder and Toner were professional villains, they made plans, they didn't improvise, yet the deal had been agreed to within minutes of Lew telling them he was in a hole and why. Still, they couldn't have known beforehand that he was coming to them for help, so they couldn't have anything too serious up their sleeves.

At least that was the comforting thought he took to bed with him. He didn't sleep very well but maybe that was the whisky.

Joe Nealis didn't sleep much either, partly for the same reasons as Lew but in his case thoughts of his wife played a contributory part. He wanted her to come back and he knew what he had to do to get her back – she'd made it clear enough. Her conditions were simple; give up playing, give up the club, give up his partnership with Lew Jackson. Simple conditions, easy to say and even easier to understand her motives in stating them. The trouble was, they were just about impossible to agree to.

The relationship with Lew, largely unspoken as recent conversations had proved, was difficult to define. It was particularly hard to explain it to a non-musician, to someone who hadn't spent years pounding pavements, humping a drum kit all over Greater London or driving a battered old band bus the length and breadth of the British Isles. Even to many insiders there was nothing romantic about playing gigs in poky, damp dance halls or clubs, being conned out of fees by unscrupulous promoters and agents, eating bad food, drinking too much, sleeping too little. There was nothing marvellous about having to listen to, and regularly play with, duff musicians night after night, or to have to scuffle for rent and bread money when all around you people with less education, less wit and intelligence, were watching their colour tellys with their two cars, caravans and small yachts parked outside in the drives of their semi-detached, well-mortgaged houses. And all for what? All for the return that came when, just occasionally, something indescribable, indefinable, happened on a bandstand. When everything you knew was supposed to happen, but almost never did, came together. When suddenly you were creating something totally great and which, ephemeral though it was to everyone else, stayed there, locked in your inner ear for ever. It didn't happen often but when it did all the rest faded into oblivion, all the pipes, slippers and wall-to-wall carpets in the world couldn't hold a candle to it.

It had happened for Joe several times in the past, usually with Lew, when his piano-playing and singing lifted above its usual standard and became almost sublime. It had even happened with unlikely people, the way it had with Harry Betts a few nights earlier. The trouble was there was no way he could explain any of it to Chris. Only another musician would understand and Joe couldn't talk about it to one, even someone like Harry Betts or Lew Jackson, particularly Lew. They were thoughts you kept to yourself for fear of receiving the expected raspberry such soul-searching revelations would attract for speaking the unspeakable.

By the time the evening rolled around again and Joe and Lew were face to face at the club, the thoughts which had kept them awake in the night were once more well and truly buried. After all, there is a limit to how much soul-searching a man can stand, especially when he has other things to worry about—like hangovers and close contact with criminals, to say nothing of organizing a jazz festival.

CHAPTER ELEVEN

'Are you sure?'

The fat man wiped his forehead, trying not to feel the way he always felt in Jack Reeder's presence. 'Yes,' he said.

Reeder thought for a moment. 'Where was this?'

'Kempsford Gardens, opposite the top end of Brompton Cemetery. I was going up to town but there was a fire at the corner of Old Brompton Road and Warwick Road so I made a detour. I recognized Mr Toner's car because I supplied it. I knew the number, you see.'

'What about the number of the other car?'

'Didn't get all of it, Mr Reeder, just part of it.'

'Write it down. Dark blue, you said.'

'That's right,' the fat man said, as he scribbled on a piece of paper. 'I hope I did right, coming to tell you, Mr Reeder.'

'Anything else?' Reeder asked, not offering the praise the fat man clearly wanted.

'No, I don't think so, only . . .'

'Only what?'

'That club in Montserrat Road, it's one of your properties, isn't it?'

'Yes, what about it?'

'I was in there a while back. That copper was

there.'

'Which copper?'

'Blackstone.'

'Blackstone?'

'Yes.'

'Was he now,' Reeder said, thoughtfully.

'Yes, seemed real matey with the owner. That slag the Honeydripper was hanging about as well.' There was silence in the room before the fat man stood up. 'Well, I'll be on my way, Mr Reeder.'

Reeder nodded. 'Yes, okay.'

At the door the other man paused. 'About the rent. You're putting it up fifteen per cent.'

'What of it?' Reeder snapped, his voice harsh.

'Nothing, nothing, Mr Reeder. Very reasonable. Very reasonable.' The fat man hastily opened the door and disappeared.

Reeder stared at the open door for a few moments. Then the shape of one of his bodyguards filled the opening as he reached in to close the door. Reeder beckoned the man in. 'I think we might have a problem there, Reg,' he said. 'Very conversational, our fat friend is getting.'

'Yes, Mr Reeder.'

'You'd better take a ride over to Vauxhall and see if you can't do something about it.'

'Yes, Mr Reeder. Permanent?'

Reeder thought for a moment. It was helpful having eyes and ears close to the ground and the used car dealer had been useful over the years, but this was the first time he'd brought information about anyone important in the hierarchy. Indeed, it wasn't possible to get any more important than Sid Toner. Unless it was Jack Reeder himself. That was the worrying part. If he let the fat man get away with informing on Toner, valuable though the information might be, it could very well give him ideas. If he decided to inform on Reeder himself there wasn't anywhere such information could go except to rival gangs or, the biggest rival of them all, the police. He ran through the number of operations for which the fat man had supplied the wheels. It was a long list. Then there was the stolen car racket, to say nothing of the container lorry swindles. He must be slipping, he thought to himself, letting one man get so involved, be so well informed. He nodded his head slowly at the bodyguard who was waiting, impassively, for an answer to his question. 'Permanent, Reg,' Reeder said.

'Shall I take Alfie or do you want me to handle it myself?'

Reeder glanced at his watch. It was four o'clock in the afternoon, which always seemed a safe time. 'Take Alfie but make it fast. I want you back here before seven.'

The bodyguard closed the door quietly and nodded to his partner, who followed him down the stairs and out of the building. They took one of the firm's cars part of the way, which allowed them to decide on a plan. When they reached Clapham Common they turned off and parked carefully, walked a couple of streets, then nicked a motor someone had been foolish enough to leave unlocked outside an ante-natal clinic. It was a six-year-old Marina, very rusty and just right for the job.

The used car lot at Vauxhall was tucked away behind the gasworks whose holders had featured in a few hundred cricket commentaries from the Oval. On one side they looked down on an area of grass dotted with a few men in white. The other side looked down on a corrugated asbestos-roofed, open-sided shed filled with motor cars. Beyond the shed was a rising, scrambled heap of rusting cars, partially broken, all the re-usable bits removed, all ready and waiting to be re-cycled.

The fat man was having a restoring pull from a can of lager he'd taken from the fridge in his glass-sided office when he saw the old Marina pull up alongside. He belched loudly, tossed the can in the waste-basket and went outside to do business. He was within arm's reach of the big man who stepped from the car before he recognized him. It took very little time for the reason for the man's presence to register, but even so it was too long. He was whisked inside the Marina and the car was moving before he had time to yell. The car didn't go back out on

89

to the road but went instead through the gates at the back of the compound, along a path between mounds of dead motor cars where it stopped. As it reappeared from between the mounds there were just two men sitting in the front seats; of the fat man there was no sign whatsoever.

The car stopped beside a man who was standing smoking by a massive, metal-sided pit. The passenger climbed out.

'Hello, Reg,' the smoker said.

'Bert. Little job for you.'

'What's that?'

The big man jerked a thumb at the Marina. 'We need it to go missing a bit sharpish.'

'Right, we'll break it up for you.'

'No, not that way. This has to be very final. Put it in the crusher.'

The man threw his cigarette end away. 'If you say so, Reg.'

'I do,' the big man agreed.

'I'll do it in about an hour, that do?'

'Why not now?'

'We've bust a drive chain. One's on its way here. . . .' He broke off as a clapped-out van wheezed up behind the Marina. 'Here it comes,' the man went on as a thin, spotty youth in greasy overalls clambered out of the van, a cardboard box in his hands. 'Take us half an hour to fit the chain then we'll be off. Put your car in first. Right?'

The big man nodded. 'Right,' he said. He

90

nodded his head at the driver of the Marina, who climbed out and joined him. 'Be done in an hour,' he told him.

The other man glanced at his watch. 'It's past six already,' he said. 'We'd better be on our way. Mr Reeder'll get a bit irate if we're not back before it's time for him to go home.'

His partner nodded and turned to the man who had started working on the driving mechanism of the crushing plant. 'No mistakes, now,' he said warningly.

The man looked up, a fresh cigarette clenched in his lips. He shook his head. 'Don't worry, Reg,' he mumbled. 'By half-past seven it'll be with those.' He jerked his head, the cigarette pointing at a small mountain of fifteen-inch cubes of metal that had once been motor cars.

The big man nodded and, with his partner, walked off down the metal-strewn path towards the used car lot.

Behind them, the man and the youth worked in silence for a little longer, then the man threw away his cigarette with an exasperated snort. 'Bleeding thing won't look at it,' he said. 'You sure you got the right chain?'

'I got what you said I had to get, Bert,' the youth whined.

'Well, it doesn't bleeding well fit. You'll have to go back for another one.'

'They'll be shut.'

'Well, first thing in the morning then.' He

looked at the Marina and shook his head. With luck, they'd have it in the crusher by nine the next morning. Reg wouldn't be any wiser unless he showed up before nine. He glanced at the youth. 'Take this car and park it down the far end, behind those old storage silos,' he told him.

He walked away, leaving the youth to do as he had ordered. He heard the engine start up but didn't look round and so didn't see the youth, who hadn't heard the conversation with Reg and who had no idea who Reg was anyway, take the car and park it somewhere else. There was a loose fence panel through which the youth occasionally took cars when he needed a set of wheels for the evening. He needed a set that evening, he had a date with a bird from out Catford way, and the Marina, rusty or not, seemed just the job. Certainly the back seat was big enough for what he had in mind. It occurred to the youth that the car might be hot but that was no problem. He'd fit a different set of plates before he took it out. That way everything would be as safe as houses and by morning no one would know anything had happened.

CHAPTER TWELVE

'Christ Almighty, there's enough electronic equipment here to start up a space factory.'

'Or even stage a rock concert.'

Lew Jackson and Joe Nealis were standing back-stage at the Town Hall surveying crate after crate of miscellaneous equipment which had been arriving over the past few days.

'How did we manage in the old days?' Joe asked. 'I don't ever remember having anything like this. If there was a mike where we played we used it, and if there wasn't we did without. Nobody ever told us we couldn't be heard.'

'More often than not they told us we played too loud,' Lew agreed.

'You don't suppose we've hired The Who by mistake, do you?'

'I don't think even Jack Reeder could afford them.'

Nealis frowned at being reminded who were their backers in the venture, and Lew cursed himself for reminding Joe of the sore point they had been skirting cautiously during the last few days. Now, with little over a week to the opening of the festival, wasn't a good time to risk creating a rift. Fortunately their conversation was interrupted when the door to the street banged open and three men walked in.

With the light behind them it was only the short, broad shape of the man in the middle which identified him as the man they had just been discussing.

'Everything going well?' Jack Reeder asked.

'Well enough,' Lew said. Nealis turned away, becoming suddenly busy reading labels on crates.

'What's all this lot then?' Reeder asked.

'Amplifiers, loudspeakers, microphones, control panel, lighting, you name it and it's here.'

'Need a hand shifting it?'

'I'll get a couple of lads over from the club.'

'Now, now, remember our arrangement. We'll supply the labour.' Reeder turned to one of his large companions. 'Get some of the boys over, Reg, see our friends here don't strain themselves.'

Lew shrugged his shoulders and looked for Joe, who had wandered further away and was opening and closing doors aimlessly. 'I'm off, mate,' Lew called. 'Coming?'

Joe turned and came across the dusty floor. 'Right,' he said. He glanced at Reeder. 'Better put some of this stuff in the basement for a few days?'

'Basement? Why?' Reeder's voice was curt.

'It's valuable, delicate equipment and there's a dog show on here before we can start setting things up. We don't want the little darlings

94

peeing over everything, do we?'

Reeder nodded, apparently surprised at the news. 'See to it, Reg,' he ordered.

'There's a trap door over there for small stuff and a goods lift back along the passage,' Joe told Reg, helpfully.

The big man nodded. 'Thanks,' he said.

After Joe and Lew had left Reeder looked at the two big men and grinned humourlessly. 'Good of them to tell us about the basement.'

'Just so long as they don't go down there themselves,' Reg said.

Reeder nodded. 'See that they don't.' He glanced at the packing crates. 'Get some of the boys over, Reg. Alfie can stay with me.'

'Yes, Mr Reeder.'

At the stage door, Reeder waited for Alfie to open the door of the Mercedes before crossing the pavement. He was feeling a shade nervous today. Nothing to worry about – probably the usual nerves before a big job. From the back of the Mercedes he glanced at the two buildings adjoining the Town Hall, one on either side, then at the shop beyond. He smiled tightly as the car pulled away, then his face resumed its usual, expressionless state. He didn't notice the man with a sallow, pinched face watching him from the doorway of a chemist's shop. The man had one hand tucked under his jacket where, from time to time, he gently massaged his ailing stomach. He popped an antacid tablet into his mouth and thought about what he had just seen. Could be something, could be nothing. You never could tell with police work.

A couple of streets away, Joe Nealis finally caught up with Lew Jackson. 'I don't like it,' he said.

'What?'

'Him. He's being too bloody helpful by half.'

'Maybe he's mellowing. Seen the light and we're the first to benefit from his new-found desire to bring a little happiness into the lives of his parishioners.'

'Balls,' Nealis said, but he didn't seem interested in pursuing the topic.

Lew glanced at his watch. 'I'm hungry,' he said. 'Fancy a plate of curry?'

'I thought you were on a diet. Anyway, I see enough of the muck we serve every night. I don't want to eat it in the middle of the day.'

'Not ours, I was thinking about some of Jumbo Patel's.'

'Okay, lead on.'

Jumbo Patel's Taj Mahal takeaway was a bright drop in an ocean of dross and peeling paint. Everything about the shop gleamed – the paintwork, inside and out, the floor, the glass-topped counter, the windows, the door knocker, Jumbo's teeth, his wife's hair. Jumbo was a small man, no more than five feet one or two and birdlike in manner and movements. He had been in England for over twenty years, most of them in Putney, and could speak accentless English when pressed. He had, however, learned that it was safer to speak with the accent of his homeland because it brought him less attention and, hence, less trouble than if he spoke English as well as, if not better than, the natives. There were a few people for whom he dropped his phoney accent, Lew and Joe among them.

'We'll split a chicken Tandoori,' Lew told him after a short discussion with Joe. 'A large helping of Biriani rice and a couple of Samosas.'

'How many calories in that lot?' Joe asked.

'You're never slimming, Lew,' Jumbo said.

'I'll sweat it off tonight,' Lew told them both. 'Speaking of which, we'd better get this lot down and go back for a run-through.'

'Since when did we need to rehearse?'

'Do you know how long it's been since we played together?'

'A few weeks.'

'It's over four months.'

'Is it?'

'It is.'

'My word, doesn't time fly when you're enjoying yourself.'

'Busy?' Jumbo asked.

'Very.'

'I heard you were holding a festival of music at the Town Hall.'

'That's right.'

97

'All your kind of music, I expect.'

'Yes, not a sitar in sight, I'm afraid, old son.'

'Ah, well, perhaps one day there will be something with which my spirit can commune.'

'Who knows, stranger things have happened. In the meantime no doubt a couple of old friends like us can prevail upon you to stick a poster in your window.'

'Of course you can,' Patel said as he went through a curtained-off opening to set their order in motion.

With the Tandoori chicken needing some time to prepare Lew and Joe decided a quick visit to the Red Lion wouldn't go amiss. Although the saloon bar was filled with its usual lunchtime crowd, the lounge was almost empty so Lew headed in there. Three people were sitting at a table against the far wall, and as the two men came in they gave three half-hearted waves. Lew recognized Honey at once and, after a moment, her two brothers, Dwight and Winston. Joe ordered drinks for himself and Lew and told the barmaid to set up another round for the three Jamaicans. He carried their drinks across, carefully leaving his own on the bar in case he wasn't welcome. The Honeydripper took the opportunity to slide out of her seat and go across to the bar where Lew was chatting up the barmaid who was new, very young, very blonde and seemed to think she knew him. When the thin, black girl came up and kissed Lew the barmaid lost interest and wandered through into the saloon bar. It occurred to Lew that he had been receiving rather a lot of kisses from Honey recently and remembered, uneasily, Joe's remarks about her regarding him in a different light from most of her customers.

'Hi, Lew,'

'Hi, Honey.' Lew nodded at her brothers. 'Family gathering?'

'I've just been telling them about the record date being off until Eddie Lester gets back from Hong Kong.'

'You reckon he'll still do it?'

The Honeydripper frowned. 'I can't see why not.'

'Maybe you're right,' Lew said, seeing no reason why he should cast gloom and despondency into the air. He thought guiltily of his regularly postponed offer. 'Look, Joe and I are going back to the club in about half an hour, we have some numbers to run through. Come along and we'll try a couple of things with you.'

'You mean it, Lew?'

He grinned. 'This time, yes.'

She leaned forward and kissed him on the lips with considerable warmth. Joe came up to the bar at that moment and eyed Lew with an odd expression on his face.

'Honey's coming back to the club with us. We'll run through a couple of numbers with her.'

'And with Dwight and Winston,' Joe said.

'Oh?'

'I beat you to it. I thought it was time a few promises were fulfilled.'

'See you later, Honey,' Lew said as the girl rejoined her brothers. 'You crafty sod,' he went on to his partner.

'Meaning what?'

'You want a bed warmer, after all.'

'That's not it at all,' Joe said tightly.

'Well, whatever it is, be warned,' Lew said. 'My dear old mum, God bless her whether she's with him or in the other place, didn't tell me a lot about women but I know enough not to try to set up a permanent relationship with a whore.'

'Don't talk about Honey that way.'

Lew peered at his partner in surprise. 'What's biting you?'

'She's a nice girl. . . .'

'Nice girl? Christ, mate, she's on the game.'

'Bloody hell, Lew, what has that got to do with it? She's honest, kind-hearted, she's got a soft spot for you . . .'

'For me?'

'. . . as I've told you already.'

'I'm beginning to think the soft spot is between your ears, old son.'

Joe blinked several times but didn't answer. He glanced across the room to where the girl was talking animatedly to Dwight and Winston. He thought about pursuing the argument, then changed his mind, for no better reason than that he didn't know why he was reacting the way he was. Up to a few days before he'd found the Honeydripper a minor irritant. Now, suddenly, he was thinking about her in a different way. He decided it was a reaction against the way she appeared to feel about Lew. It wasn't the first time a young woman had behaved that way – particularly in the early days, when Lew's off-hand manner and cut-glass accent had made him stand out against the backdrop of the majority of the other musicians on the road. Now, although the off-handedness remained, the accent had blurred and thickened, like his waistline, and the women were less interested. For a moment Joe found himself wondering why he stuck it out, running the club almost single-handed while Lew swanned around trying to find a crack in the wall that separated him from the big time. Then he shrugged his shoulders—he'd stuck it this long, there didn't seem much point in rocking the boat just because Lew was being his usual cold-blooded self over a woman. He swallowed the remains of his glass of beer.

'Another?' Lew asked.

'Half.'

Lew called for the barmaid who came back, took their orders and when she had deposited their refilled glasses on the bar stayed, eyeing

Lew carefully. 'You're a musician,' she said, eventually.

'So it has been rumoured, darling.'

'I saw you at that club in Montserrat Road last Christmas.'

'You could have done. I had the pleasure of appearing there about that time.'

'Bit tatty, I thought.'

'Him or the club?' Joe asked interestedly.

'Oh, the club,' she said seriously. 'I thought you were quite good. My boyfriend said you reminded him of Leon Redbone.'

'I don't remember him wearing a pith helmet that time,' Joe said.

'Pardon?'

He shook his head. 'Nothing. Tell your boyfriend we're having a jazz festival, Bank Holiday weekend.'

'He's not my boyfriend any more,' the barmaid said.

'Oh dear, what a shame.'

'Good thing too,' she went on. 'Now that he's in trouble with the police.'

'Tut, tut. What did he do, steal a hubcap off a car?'

'No, something serious.'

'Off a moving car?'

'No. He nicked a car and the police stopped him for speeding.'

'How absolutely dreadful,' Lew said, finishing his drink and edging away from the bar.

'Yes, isn't it? Especially when they found a body in the boot.'

Joe raised an eyebrow. 'What kind of body?'

'A dead one.'

'Dog, cat or rabbit?'

'A man.'

'What exciting lives you young people lead,' Lew said as he headed for the door, leaving Joe to hastily swallow his drink and follow.

Outside Nealis caught up with Lew. 'Lost your sense of humour?' he asked.

'I don't like people telling me my club's tatty.'

'It's our club, not yours, and it *is* tatty.'

'Coming from you I can take it, coming from me I can take it, but coming from some bit of a kid who's barely out of blue serge bloomers I take exception.'

'You're annoyed because her boyfriend said he thought you were like Leon Redbone.'

'I can see no reason to worry over the opinion of someone who steals a car without checking to see if there's anything dead in the boot.'

Joe grinned and refrained from further comment. By the time they had picked up their lunch from Jumbo Patel and walked back to the club Lew had forgotten about the conversation with the girl. As soon as they had eaten they began running through one or two of the old numbers they thought of as their basic repetoire. They were just finishing *How Long, How Long Blues* when the Honeydripper arrived with her brothers who had been home, Dwight to collect his conga drum and Winston his guitar.

At Lew's suggestion they started with *Can't Stop Rafta Now*, the song Honey had sung for Eddie Lester, then he asked her to try *When a Woman Loves a Man*. Honey didn't know the song, so he ran through the verse and a couple of choruses himself while Joe ferreted about for a copy of the music with words. When he found one she tried the number and sounded quite good. The second time they ran it through she was better and by the fourth time was beginning to feel the song and put something of herself into the lyric. Dwight and Winston played well and all five of them enjoyed themselves. A couple more songs were tried, and by the time they were over Lew had decided he would definitely use Honey at the club. A try-out on a Tuesday or Thursday to start with—both notoriously dead nights, but with big enough audiences to make her feel she was getting a fair deal and not so big it would frighten her.

Before any of them realized, it was six o'clock and the two young men left, Dwight to go on late shift at the bus depot and Winston to report to his probation officer. The Honeydripper hung around, clearly expecting Lew to make some suggestion for the rest of the evening, but when none was forthcoming she left reluctantly.

Joe Nealis glanced at his watch. 'I need a shave and a bath,' he announced. 'Are you staying here until we open?'

'I might. You carry on, if I pop home I'll lock up and be back before Oscar gets here.'

'Right,' Joe said. He went up the stairs, the door banging shut behind him.

Lew, still sitting at the piano, ran through *Dinah*, taking the tune at a slow, reflective pace, not singing the words which didn't hang too easily at that tempo. He found he was more relaxed than he had been for some time and quite happily wandered through half a dozen more songs. He was still playing when Oscar, the barman, arrived to set up for the night and Lew decided it was too late to go home. He went through to the toilets and washed his face and hands in the cracked, stained basin.

Back in the bar he had a scotch and soda, listening to the two kitchen hands arguing as they set about heating up last night's curry. The rising smell, coming on top of what he'd eaten for lunch, made him feel slightly ill so he had another drink. The evening was in full swing, the guest band, a six-piece outfit playing out-of-date Dixieland blasting away to the apparent delight of the audience, before Joe came back.

When it was time for Lew's set his mood had drifted into one of mild, unaccountable depression. Coupled with Joe for once failing to maintain good time-keeping, it resulted in a dull, dreary thirty minutes of music. The fact that the audience didn't seem to notice, and applauded enthusiastically, in no way made up for the gloom they all felt when it was time to knock off for the night. By the time the club was empty of punters and staff, both Lew and Joe were pleased to lock up and go home. Neither commented on the evening's poor musical results, although both were aware that their rehearsal and the entertaining session with Honey and her brothers had led them to expect better. They'd both been around long enough to know that post-mortems didn't help. If something was dead it was best forgotten.

CHAPTER THIRTEEN

The report on the post-mortem on Gus Jacobs, former used car dealer of Vauxhall, gourmand and incipient alcoholic, was sitting neatly in the middle of Detective-Chief Superintendent George Blackstone's otherwise empty desk. Periodically the detective moved it a fraction of an inch to one side, then back again, as if this gentle stirring might result in some daylight suddenly beaming from its cold-blooded pages. Not that he was in any doubt about the cause of Gus's death. His skull had been smashed in with

106

a heavy metal object, probably a rusty iron bar. There were several pages of miscellaneous medical claptrap regarding the state of health of the victim at the time of his death, none of which interested Blackstone in the slightest. He needed something which would point him in the right direction or, to be precise, since he was reasonably sure where to look for the killer, something upon which he could build a case.

'Any news on Bert Dixon?' he asked.

His sergeant raised a weary head and turned to survey his superior officer with a red-tinged eye. 'No, sir.'

Bert Dixon was the man who operated the scrap-yard where Blackstone had satisfied himself the murder had been committed. 'A creep like that can't have gone far, for God's sake.'

'Yes, sir,' said his sergeant.

'We'll have to let that little toe-rag go soon, Green.'

The sergeant, whose name wasn't Green, nodded. The spotty, grease-stained youth who had stolen the car in which Gus Jacobs's body had been found was becoming something of a burden. It wasn't the usual tale of someone refusing to co-operate—quite the reverse in fact. The youth hadn't stopped talking from the moment he had regained consciousness after fainting at the sight which greeted him when an equally astonished constable had opened up the boot of the Marina along the A23 a few nights earlier. So far the youth had informed on seventeen people including his employer, Bert Dixon, his own father and two of his brothers. It was only the fact that his mother had gone to what was probably a much-welcomed early grave that had prevented him dropping her in it too.

'If we do, we'll have to give the press something.'

Blackstone nodded grimly. So far they'd managed to keep things quiet. He was sure there had been a criminal cock-up and the longer he kept it to himself the better his chance of spreading alarm and despondency among the ranks of the fraternity. He heaved himself upright. 'I think it's time for another word with our jazz club-owning friend,' he announced. 'That black whore as well, she was with Gus the last time we saw him.' The sergeant frowned, having forgotten all about the evening he had been taken to the South Bank Jazz Club by his chief. He stood up wearily but sank back in relieved surprise when Blackstone shook his head. 'No, you stay here, have another go at Spotty while I'm out. We'll think about letting him go tomorrow, after I've made a few preparations.'

The sergeant stared at the closed door and felt a tiny glimmer of hope. Maybe he was about to get his long-awaited transfer. He wondered if the time was right to let drop another little hint of his unreliability. It was a dangerous game— he had to make himself out to be just sufficiently unreliable to get away from Blackstone, but not so much that he earned a reprimand. He decided to hang on another couple of days, see how things went after Gus Jacob's death became public knowledge.

It didn't surprise George Blackstone when Lew Jackson didn't welcome him with open arms when he arrived at the club. Lew was on the point of a nervous collapse and didn't care who knew it. With only a matter of days to go before his festival things were hotting up and he was coping with the pressure with all the grace of a Chelsea supporter whose team had just lost ten-nil to Fulham.

'Bastards,' he was screaming as Blackstone lumbered down the stairs. 'Bloody sodding bastards.' A large tin ashtray was hurled across the room to ricochet off the wall before rolling noisily around in ever-decreasing circles, finally to expire in a machine-gun-like rattle. 'Sods,' Lew said, a little more quietly. Oscar the barman moved to pick up the ash-tray, but stopped when he saw Blackstone's large left foot a few inches from it. The two kitchen hands, both smelling faintly of curry, stood by helplessly. As things had spiralled up towards the big day, Lew had co-opted everyone he could find to help with his arrangements. In this case, everyone he could find amounted to Oscar and the two curry-ladlers, none of whom had any experience of doing anything remotely like organizing a jazz festival. In fact, one of the kitchen hands couldn't even read or write, something Lew discovered after the unfortunate lad had spent an entire afternoon sticking up posters and parking zone signs in the vicinity of the Town Hall. Almost without exception the signs were upside-down and Lew had been obliged to spend most of the night sticking additional signs over the originals. It hadn't pleased him one little bit. Now, at the last moment, he had discovered that one of the caterers, Charlie Cheshire, the Cheese Sandwich Specialist from Balham High Road, had been closed down by the local health inspector for unspecified reasons.

Lew glowered at the two kitchen hands. 'You'll have to step in,' he told them.

'What? Make ten thousand cheese sandwiches? Bloody hell, it isn't possible, Lew.'

'Well, make as many as you can.'

'But we're already having to make half a ton of curry.'

'I can't help it if Jumbo Patel's on his holidays. Just get some bread and cheese ordered and I'll see if I can't hire somebody to help you. Some of the girls from the pickle factory might be interested in making a few extra quid.' He turned and saw the policeman.

'Oh, Jesus Christ, that's all I need.'

'Now, now,' Blackstone said politely. 'Just a few questions.'

Lew opened his mouth to protest but thought better of it. He nodded instead towards the office. 'Okay, in there but I'd appreciate it if you could cut it short. I have a lot to do.'

'The police never waste the time of the law-abiding public,' Blackstone said, without appearing to lie.

In the office, there was barely room to breathe and both men had to stand. 'Well?' Lew asked.

Blackstone asked him about the fat used car dealer from Vauxhall, and Lew was able to convince him that he hadn't seen the man before or since the minor ruckus the night he had first met Blackstone himself.

'What about the whore?' Blackstone asked.

'Honey?' Lew asked, feeling mildly resentful at the policeman's terminology, accurate though it was. 'What about her?'

'Did she know him?'

'She met him here for the first time that same night.'

'That's what she told you, is it?'

'Yes, anyway, ask her yourself.'

'I'd like to but I can't find her. I've wasted a few hours today looking for her. Seems she's hopped it.'

'Hopped it?'

'Gone.'

'Gone?'

'Disappeared.'

'Disappeared?'

'Surprising there's an echo in here, seeing how crowded it is.'

Lew took a deep breath. 'Let's start again. Tell me about Honey.'

'She isn't at her flat and, according to her brothers, she hasn't been home either.'

'Since when?'

Blackstone consulted his notebook. 'Last Tuesday.'

Lew thought hard and remembered that was the day they'd had the rehearsal with the girl and her two brothers. He told Blackstone and realized the big man was nodding his agreement as he read from his notebook. Blackstone looked up, saw Lew's expression, and waved the notebook gently in the air. 'That concurs with statements made by the girl's brothers. Seems they left here before she did, which means you and your partner were the last people to see her. As far as we know,' he added darkly.

Lew was silent, trying hard to reconcile what he was hearing. 'There can't be anything wrong,' he said. 'She's probably gone away for a few days.'

'Without telling anyone?'

Lew frowned. 'Are you saying something's happened to her?'

'No, and I can't say I'm all that interested if it

has. Her kind ask for trouble. No, all I want is to ask her some questions about Gus Jacobs.'

'I'll see what I can find out,' Lew said. 'Not for your benefit,' he added. 'Honey's a friend, which is a lot more than you are.'

'Knowing things like that keeps me happy,' Blackstone said as he eased his way out of the office.

Lew followed him across the floor towards the stairs but both were brought to an abrupt halt when the street door crashed open and a small, immensely fat body, swathed in what seemed like a few dozen yards of purple parachute material, began to descend the stairs. While most people had to come at least five steps down before their heads came into view, this one needed only three steps. The woman was barely as tall as she was wide and her face, frowning in concentration as she negotiated the staircase, was round, treble-chinned and shining black. Lew recognized her instantly—it was one of the stars of his festival. Big Mama Richards, blues singer extraordinaire, man-eater and patent-medicine nut, had arrived.

'Jesus Christ, lover,' she yelled when she saw Lew staring at her. 'I ain't been in a cellar like this since the day they took away my licence. Thought these places went out with Boss Pendergast.'

Lew helped her down the last few steps and introduced himself, carefully ignoring

Blackstone who was edging round trying to get a foot on the stairs. Unfortunately, Big Mama's descent had taken a lot out of her and she collapsed on to the bottom step, her breath wheezing heavily. 'Christ, lover, I'll have to stop smoking those Goddamn cigars. Either that or stop fucking before noon.' She shrieked with laughter and almost rolled off the step.

Lew swallowed and risked a question. 'What are you doing here? I mean, you're very welcome but the festival doesn't start for another three days.'

'Christ, lover, I know that. I'm playing out at some goddam asshole joint called Snape Meltings but I thought I'd drop off and see what the hell we're gonna do at your festival.'

'Maltings,' Lew corrected.

Big Mama didn't notice the correction. She had just become aware of the big policeman. 'Well, well, lover, who's the big boy? Introduce me, introduce me.'

'George Blackstone,' Lew said, unwillingly. 'Big Mama Richards.'

'You a musician, lover? Got to admit you don't look like one.'

'I, madam, am a police officer,' Blackstone said stiffly.

'Jesus Christ. A real London cop. Here, let me get up.' The fat little woman reached up one hand to Lew, the other to Blackstone. Lew took the hand and pulled and when Blackstone didn't

114

offer a similar aid the singer seized hold of his trouser leg and heaved herself upright, the strain on her almost as great as the strain on Blackstone's braces.

The indignity proved too much for the policeman, who forced his way past the little woman and made a rapid ascent of the staircase.

'Hey, lover, what's your hurry?' Big Mama yelled, but the only answer was a resounding crash as the door slammed shut. 'Hell now, what did I do?' she complained to Lew.

'He has a criminal to catch,' Lew told her, not out of any desire to explain Blackstone's actions but in order not to alienate one of his big-name attractions.

'That right? Will he be back?'

Lew glanced up the stairs. 'I have a feeling he will,' he said.

For the next hour, until Big Mama had to be pushed and pulled up the stairs by Lew and Oscar the barman and helped into a waiting taxi, he was totally involved in setting up a programme of songs and determining the kind of accompanying group she wanted for her two performances, on the Saturday and Sunday nights. It wasn't until he had staggered, breathless, down to the office after she had gone that he was able to think again about the policeman's visit. He wasn't too clear about the reason for it. The used car dealer from Vauxhall obviously had something to do with it, but there seemed nothing to link him with the Honeydripper. He wondered why she had gone off without telling anyone. He realized he was thinking from a stand-point of knowing nothing about her personal life. With that in mind there was, equally, no reason why she should have told anyone anything. Except, as far as he could gather, she had always been close to her brothers, particularly Dwight and Winston. It seemed odd. He shrugged. It really wasn't his business.

A couple of hours later he decided he needed a wash, a shave and a change of clothes before the evening's work began. He went up the stairs and into the fading sunlight. He had just unlocked the door of his old Granada when something hard pressed into his back and a voice, close to his ear, whispered the words he'd heard used in countless old movies and new television shows but had never before heard spoken in earnest.

'This is a gun,' he was told. 'Do as you're told and you won't get hurt.'

CHAPTER FOURTEEN

'Christ, what's that smell?'

'Dogs.'

'Dogs?'

'They're having a dog show upstairs.'

'Bloody hell.'

'At least it's better than bleeding hamsters,' a little man in a boiler suit put in.

The basement of the Town Hall was dark, musty and littered with packing cases and crates, some open, others still nailed tightly. Interspersed among the clutter were several men. Jack Reeder's bodyguards, Reg and Alfie, were there as was the little man in the boiler suit who answered to the name of Herbie; a heavy-set man with tattooed ear lobes and an impenetrable accent all the Londoners had long since given up trying to understand; a bad-tempered Welshman, a chain-smoking Mancunian and a few others. None of the out-of-towners was in a very good humour, brought about through a combination of not enough freedom of movement, too little alcohol, no women and, in the case of the man from Cardiff, the inability to sing in his bath.

A heavy, steel-framed door opened with a complaining screech and the grey-clad figure of Sid Toner came into the basement. He nodded at the assembled mob and got straight down to business by unfolding a carefully drawn blueprint. Everyone listened in silence. When he finished he asked for questions, answered two from the chain-smoker and one from the Welshman. Then he left them to study the plan and crossed to where little Herbie and the two bodyguards were standing at an accommodating distance as befitted their lack of status in the presence of the team of specialists.

'Where's Mr Reeder?' Toner asked Reg.

The big man looked at him enquiringly and Sid realized he had made a tactical error. He couldn't account for it but during the past few days he had seen much less of Jack Reeder than was usual, especially immediately prior to a big job like this one. It disturbed him a little—it was usually the other way around. He would see Reeder when it suited him and when it didn't he went his own way. The fact that Reeder was the boss was something which didn't usually enter into things. 'I understood he was coming here today,' he said, covering his lapse. 'Must have got the arrangements mixed up.'

He turned as the men gathered around the plan straightened up. 'Any questions?' he asked again.

He got a mumbled chorus he took to mean they hadn't, and a few minutes later the men began to drift out of the basement up the stairs into the back-stage area. From there, at two-minute intervals, they entered the main hall where row upon row of cages were filled with dogs of all sizes, some barking, others yelping or howling or staring in gloomy silence over their well-coiffured co-exhibits. Some of the dogs had had their hair done too.

The big Geordie was the last of the out-of-towners to leave, and as he passed between two Red Setters and their owners who were comparing notes on worming techniques he stood on a foot. 'Sorreah,' he rumbled.

'Okay,' the man said. After the Geordie had disappeared, the man whose foot had received his full, crushing weight wandered in the same direction, one hand rubbing against his stomach which was acting up again. Talk about a dog's life, he thought to himself, a policeman's lot is a bloody sight worse. All he'd done was come in here for a quiet hour away from Detective-Chief-Superintendent George Blackstone and what did he do but stumble over one of the missing specialists. He reached the steps of the Town Hall but could see no sign of the man with the tattooed ear lobes. It wouldn't please Blackstone very much at all. The thin man grinned suddenly. That meant he had two things up his sleeve until the time was right to drop a little bit of information in the Chief's ear. He wandered along the street, his incipient ulcer forgotten as he tried to decide where he would like his transfer to take him. Brighton would be

119

nice, not too much sweat there, just the occasional foray with an over-inebriated actor or maybe a run-in with the local garden-gnome-stealing fraternity. Yes, Brighton would do just fine.

He reached a telephone kiosk and went in to dial the station to report in. When he was put through to Blackstone he wasn't given time to say anything but was ordered, curtly, to get his arse into the office a bit sharpish. He came out of the kiosk with his hand back inside the waistband of his trousers. Blackstone had been even more irascible than usual. Something, clearly, was on his mind, and the detective-sergeant had a sinking feeling that it wasn't his transfer.

CHAPTER FIFTEEN

'For God's sake, it's you. Jesus, but you scared me there for a minute,' Lew said.

'Shut up and drive,' he was told. 'This isn't no joke, man.'

Lew frowned at the tone of voice. It sounded serious. He looked from Dwight, who was holding the pistol, to Winston who was carrying a small but dangerous-looking cosh. They both appeared highly nervous. 'What's up?' he asked.

'Drive, I said.'

'Okay, okay. I'll drive.' He turned and started the Granada. 'Where to?'

'What?'

'Where shall I drive?'

There was silence and, glancing up into the rear-view mirror, he saw the two young men exchange uncertain glances. Clearly, whatever they were up to they hadn't worked out their plans with any great degree of thoroughness. 'Honey's, go to Honey's place,' Dwight said after a moment.

'Honey's?'

'Yes, man, that's where. You know where that is, don't you?' There was definite anger in his tone and Lew engaged gear and drove cautiously away without further debate. There was no point in antagonizing someone who was already angry and edgy, especially when he was holding a gun.

Honey's flat looked generally as it had on the occasion of his last visit there, but the atmosphere differed, partially because of the bright sunlight which replaced the subdued lighting and partly from the threatening presence of the two tall young men. 'Okay, where is she?' Dwight asked.

'I don't know where she is.'

'She's missing, man.'

'I know she is.'

'There, see, he knows,' Winston put in

excitedly.

'Of course I know, I've had Blackstone on my neck.'

'What else do you know?'

'Nothing.'

Dwight brandished the pistol. 'You'd better talk,' he threatened.

In the confined space of the room Lew was able to take a better look at the gun, and to his surprise and relief he saw it was an air pistol. He began to relax a little, though not too much because he was aware that, at close range, such a weapon could cause a nasty wound or even kill if it was aimed accurately. 'Listen,' he said quietly. 'Why would I want to do anything to harm Honey? I like her, she's a nice kid.'

'You were the last to see her.'

'I was?'

'We left her at the club with you and Joe. Nobody's seen her since then.'

'Somebody must have done.'

He got two equally puzzled frowns. 'What's that mean?'

'If she's gone away on her own then someone, somewhere, will have seen her.' He hesitated. 'If something has happened to her, then, equally, somebody will have seen her.'

The logic of his argument took some time to unravel before Dwight replied. 'That somebody could still be you,' he said.

Lew nodded, relieved to note some of the

menace had left his voice. 'It isn't,' he said firmly.

'She's never gone away before without telling us,' Winston said plaintively.

Lew moved slowly towards the divan and sat down. 'Okay,' he told them. 'Let's take this one step at a time.'

For the next ten minutes they covered, in detail, the period from when they had all been together in the club until the brothers had discovered Honey wasn't around. That done, Lew realized the young men knew nothing which could be of any help in finding their sister. For one thing, it seemed he was the only one of her clients they had ever met.

'I think I'd better get back to the club,' Lew said. 'I can make a few telephone calls and see if I can find out anything.'

'There's a telephone here,' Dwight said.

Lew, who had no idea who to call and had made the statement as a means of getting away, thought quickly. 'The people I want to call have unlisted numbers. I need to be in my office.'

Dwight and Winston thought for a moment and decided there was some strength in the argument. 'We'll come with you,' Dwight told him.

'I'm going home first, you come to the club later.' He paused, seeing the doubt in their eyes. 'I'm not likely to run away, am I? After all, I haven't any need to.'

They agreed and Lew left them sitting, incongruous and slightly uncomfortable-looking in the room where their sister had earned the money to bring them to England by selling her body to countless men. As he went down the stairs Lew experienced a feeling he didn't immediately identify. He was back in his flat, shaving, when it registered. He felt guilty. Then the guilt was replaced by anger that he should think that way. He forced himself to think about the Honeydripper in logical terms. For a start, there was no reason to think anything had happened to her, although there seemed to be some strength in her brothers' opinion that she would have told them before leaving if she had gone under her own steam. As he dressed he wondered why he was bothering. He didn't owe Honey any favours and he certainly didn't owe the girl's brothers any. If she had disappeared it was the business either of the girl herself or of the police. Even so he couldn't clear his mind of the Honeydripper, and by the time he reached the club he had decided to ask around, make an announcement maybe. He was in the office when something tugged at the edge of his memory. He wasn't sure what it was and concentrated for a few minutes. He finally succeeded in bringing the thought to the surface just as Joe Nealis arrived.

'My God, what's happened?' Joe asked.

'Eh?'

'You look as if you've just been elected as a judge for the Eurovision Song Contest.'

'Nearly as bad. I've had a visitation—several in fact.'

'Explain.'

'Honey has disappeared. Seems nobody's seen her since we had that session down here last Tuesday. The police are interested and her brothers feel I might have something to do with it.'

'Oh,' Joe said, and went out of the office. He came back a few moments later with a glass of beer in one hand and a scotch and water in the other. The two men drank in silence before Joe spoke. 'Why are you taking it seriously?'

'I don't bloody well know. Look, there's something that's been bothering me. You remember when I came back from Hampstead and told you Lester had gone off to Hong Kong?'

'I'm never likely to forget it.'

'Did you tell Honey where he'd gone?'

'Why should I?'

'Then you didn't?'

'No.'

'Well, you remember the Tuesday, the day she disappeared? We met her and her brothers in the Red Lion. She came up to the bar to talk to me while you were talking to Dwight and Winston. She said she'd just been telling them Lester was in Hong Kong.'

'So?'

'So, how did she know?' Lew asked, then went on without waiting for a reply. 'There's something else. You remember the night Sid Toner came in here and you talked to him – went through *Jazz Journal* telling him who was appearing around and about?'

'Yes.'

'You said he wanted to know how I was getting on with the arrangements for the festival.'

'That's right.'

'Well, how did he know there was a festival? Did you tell him?'

'No.'

'If you didn't and I didn't, who else is left?'

'You tell me, you're the one who's playing detective.'

'Lester told him, Eddie bloody Lester.'

'Why should he?'

'Christ Almighty, stop asking me questions I can't answer.'

'Word was getting around, you'd been trying all the agencies and caterers.'

'None of which were Sid Toner's scene. No— he must have known because Lester told him.'

'Like I said, why should he?'

'Listen, take it a step at a time. First of all you and I are sitting here minding our own business, counting our losses, when Honey comes in and drops word that she's got an audition with this

126

Lester character. I do what I always do when someone mentions a man with money, I get itchy-fingered and go to see him. Quick as a flash he offers a deal I take to be a result of my charm and personality. Then, when I can't get the thing off the ground, Sid Toner shows up and asks you how I'm doing. You tell him zilch and suddenly people start having fires and other problems. Before you know it, musicians are being offered from all directions. Also, he gave you his card with an unexplained offer of help if we needed it. Suddenly, Lester hops it to Hong Kong, leaving me stuck with a need for immediate cash and a lot of it. With nowhere else to turn I go to Toner and he makes me the offer I can't refuse. Money and unlimited manpower.'

Nealis had listened carefully and now slowly nodded his head. 'I can see what you're driving at but I can't see any reason for it all. If Toner wanted to lend you money for a festival, all he had to do was walk in here and offer it.'

Lew shook his head. 'I wouldn't have taken it.'

'Wouldn't you?'

'Not from a villain like that.'

'Are you sure?'

Lew thought for a moment, then grinned. 'No, I'm not sure. But the chances are I would have thought hard and looked at it a bit more carefully than I looked at Lester's deal. As it was, by the time I went to Toner I was desperate and even his money was better than no money at all.'

'So where does all that get us?'

'I don't know, mate, but I'm going to find out. Mr Toner is up to something, something which involves me and my festival.'

'And Honey?'

'Honey?'

'All this brain work started because you think she's disappeared.'

'Right. Maybe there is a connection. Maybe she knows something and somebody has taken steps to shut her up.'

Nealis thought for a moment, his eyes blinking. 'Why did Blackstone want to see her?'

'Something to do with a slob who was in here one night. I didn't tell you about it. Some drunk Honey had picked up got stroppy and Blackstone frightened him off.'

'What was his name?'

Lew thought. 'Jacobs, I think he said.'

'Gus Jacobs? Used car dealer from Vauxhall?'

'That's right. Do you know him?'

'No, but there was a piece about him on tonight's television news. The police seem to think it's a gangland killing.'

Lew frowned. 'Do they, now? So that's why Blackstone was asking about him. Gangland killing, eh?'

'What does that knowing look mean?'

'The only gangsters I know are Sid Toner and Jack Reeder.'

'So?'

'So I've had more than my share of coincidences.'

'What are you going to do about it?'

'Ask a few questions and keep an ear to the ground.'

'If you have any brains you'll keep your head down.'

'Well I'm not. Somebody's set me up for a mug. I don't know why I've been used, but used is what I've been. I think it's time I found out why.'

'We do have a club to run, to say nothing of a festival which opens in less than seventy-two hours from now.'

'What do you want me to do?'

'Wait until it's over, then we can do something about it.'

Lew shook his head. 'Then might be too late. If my theories have any truth in them, the festival's at the heart of it all.' He stood up, suddenly grim. 'I've waited years for the chance to do this, I'm not having it screwed up by some lousy little low-life.'

'He might be lousy little low-life but Reeder has a reputation for being a bit nasty with his enemies.'

'I'll be careful,' Lew said.

'I hope you will. I wouldn't like to have to

handle the festival on my own.'

'It's nice to know I'm needed. Speaking of which I'll go and have a ripple before the punters arrive.'

Lew went out of the office and across the floor to the bandstand. He sat at the piano and began to play one of the numbers he would be playing later. He didn't need the extra run-through but had suddenly felt a need for some quiet thinking. Joe had precipitated it with his reminder that Sid Toner and Jack Reeder, particularly Reeder, could be dangerous people to cross. He was angry, there was no doubt about it. More than anything else he wanted the festival to succeed. He had to do something about the villains who seemed to be ganging up on him but at the same time where was nothing to be gained by putting himself in the firing line. After all, that wouldn't do any good to anything or anybody. It wouldn't do any good to the festival or the club. It wouldn't do any good to the missing Honey. And it certainly wouldn't do any good for Lew Jackson.

He stopped playing in the middle of a run, went to the bar and helped himself to a scotch. He glanced through the window of the office where Joe was talking on the telephone. He grinned. It wouldn't do Joe much good either, if anything happened to him. He raised his glass in a toast to his unaware partner. Good old Joe, he thought, there weren't all that many people who would have stood up to the trials and troubles of the past thirty years.

Inside the office the subject of Lew's thoughts was frowning over the telephone. 'I don't like it,' he was saying. 'Especially this tie-up with a killing.' He listened for a few moments, then nodded. 'Okay, just a little longer but we'll have to be careful, very careful.' He replaced the telephone and sat staring at the wall, then stood up and went out to set up his drums. He managed to avoid talking to Lew again before the first set. It embarrassed him, the fact that for the first time in thirty years he wasn't being honest with his partner.

CHAPTER SIXTEEN

'Bleeding hell. On the bleeding television news. Angela bleeding Rippon it was as well. A bleeding body in the bleeding boot of a stolen bleeding car pinched by some bleeding arsewipe. Oh, Jesus bleeding Christ.'

Jack Reeder was not pleased. Put another way, he was very, very angry. He fell silent and stumped back to his desk where he sat down heavily and glowered at the men in the room with him. There were the two bodyguards, Reg and Alfie, neither of whom seemed quite as big as usual, little Herbie in his customary boiler suit, and Sid Toner who was doing a nice job of blending into the grey-painted walls of the office. None of them felt very happy about being where they were at that particular moment. The silence dragged on, which was not a good sign. Reeder's outbursts of rage were fairly common and rarely resulted in anything more serious than someone, somewhere, being taken suddenly sick with a broken leg or two. On the other hand, Reeder's silences were often the prelude to physical damage of a slightly more lasting nature.

Eventually Reeder looked up to direct his eyes with some effort at the two bodyguards. 'What's the name of the toe-rag at the scrap-yard?'

'Bert Dixon.'

'Where is he?'

'He's hopped it, Mr Reeder.'

'Well, find him.'

'Yes, Mr Reeder,' Reg said, and hesitated.

'Well?'

'It's nine o'clock, Mr Reeder, getting dark outside it is.'

'So what? Get moving.'

'Yes, Mr Reeder.' Reg and Alfie headed for the door, feeling decidedly uneasy. If Mr Reeder was prepared to step into the dark streets without their comforting presence then quite clearly they had been moved to a new low on the boss's shit-list.

'And don't show your face in here until you've found him,' Reeder yelled at their retreating backs. He turned his gaze on to Herbie, who wiped his nose on the sleeve of his boiler suit and tried a tentative smile. He didn't get one in return and stood, nervously shifting his weight from one foot to another, until Reeder spoke. 'The lad who pinched the car, I think we should have a little word with him, Herbie.'

'Yes, Mr Reeder.'

'He can't know much, otherwise the jacks wouldn't have let him out on bail. Still, won't do us any harm to know just what he has told them.'

'Yes, Mr Reeder. Er. . . .'

'Yes?'

'Do you want to ask him, or do you want me to do it?'

Reeder looked down at his hands which were clenched into tight little fists. Slowly, his fingers opened and he felt some of his tension and anger fading away at the prospect of having a helpless, frightened individual on whom to work off his excess irritability. 'I'll talk to him, Herbie. Take him to the warehouse.'

'Yes, Mr Reeder.' Herbie scuttled for the door, relieved both at getting out of the boss's way and by the fact that it seemed as if someone else would be taking the brunt of Reeder's wrath.

When Herbie's footsteps had faded there was silence in Reeder's office. It wasn't a friendly silence and Sid Toner knew there was more to it than the immediate problem of the dead man who, by then, should have been re-cycled into the near-side wing of a Land Rover up at Solihull. He knew that, in some way, he was at fault but couldn't for the life of him work out why. The August Bank Holiday job was lined up with no apparent problems, the rents and rake-offs were coming in unabated, yet the atmosphere between Reeder and himself had been decidedly strained for the past few days. It was a bit alarming, especially when Reeder was being aggravated by the incompetence of the soldiers. Not that Toner's area of responsiblity extended to the front-line troops. He was the planner, the organizer, the brains. He frowned. He would have welcomed the chance to talk to his own contact, the man whose brainchild the August Bank Holiday job had been, but there was no hope of it. His contact was well away from the scene of the action. For the first time for many years, Sid Toner suddenly found himself wishing he too was far, far away.

He was about to break the silence when Reeder did it for him. 'I am not happy, Sid. I am definitely not a happy man.'

'It's an awkward one, Jack, no doubt about it. But there's nobody to tie it back to you. Apart from this Bert bloke—and as soon as Reg and

Alfie turn him up he'll be no problem.'

Reeder shook his head. 'I'm not talking about that, Sid. The whole deal's getting too complicated by half. I'm not sure I like it.'

'The big job?'

'Yes, the big job. We should have settled for something a bit less complicated and further from our own doorstep as well.'

Toner hesitated, not wanting to say what had come into his mind but aware that he needed to placate the little man behind the desk. 'It's not too late to call it off,' he said.

Reeder leaned back in his chair. 'What would it cost us if we do?'

Toner took a little notebook from his pocket and glanced at it. 'We'd have to pay the outside boys for their time and trouble and we've already laid out on materials. Apart from that there's the advances we've let Jackson pay out for the festival. Altogether we can keep the loss down to no more than ten thousand if we pull out now.'

'Ten grand, Jesus Christ. . . .'

Toner cut in hastily. 'Of course that's before the festival. It can still go ahead anyway, and if Jackson's predictions are anywhere near right we'll be able to pay everybody off and come out even. No profit maybe, but no loss either.'

Reeder nodded, seemingly mollified. 'I never thought I'd see the day when I'd end up promoting a bleeding jazz concert,' he said.

Toner was relieved to recognize the tone of voice which suggested the worst had past. 'Might have its uses in the future,' he said. 'A nice respectable front, could come in handy.'

Reeder nodded, his mind on other things. He was not a very sophisticated man and was having difficulty in deciding just how to raise the matter of Sid Toner's mysterious midnight meetings with an unknown man in a dark blue Rolls-Royce. It was an awkward one for Reeder, whose upbringing was such that it never occurred to him to ask a direct question. It had also never occurred to him that the meeting might have been entirely innocent and of no significance to him. 'Nothing else to tell me, Sid?' he asked eventually.

Toner shook his head, unhappily aware that the wording of the question showed quite clearly that whatever it was that had come between himself and Reeder was still there.

Reeder stood up and crossed to the window to stare down into the alley. 'I think we need to cover a few more loose ends,' he said.

'Such as?'

'That black whore, what's her name?'

'The Honeydripper.'

'That's her. Can she cause us any trouble?'

'No. She knows the business with Eddie Lester was a fix but that won't interest the jacks. It might give Lew Jackson grounds for complaint but if it does he'll take it out on her, no one else.'

'I'm not so sure. The word is the jacks want to talk to her about Jacobs.'

'Why?' Toner asked, genuinely surprised.

'I don't know, Sid,' Reeder replied with some asperity. 'If I knew I might not be so worried. It might be nothing—you know what the coppers are like. But if she knows something. . . .' His voice trailed off.

Sid Toner hesitated, then saw a way to appease Reeder and perhaps restore the breach between them. 'Want me to find her for you, Jack?'

Reeder turned round, something like a smile on his face. 'Yes, do that, will you, Sid?' He returned to his desk and sat down again, watching as Toner crossed to the door to leave. 'Sid,' he said quietly, as his right-hand man opened the door.

'Yes, Jack?'

'We'll have a little meeting. All of us. Reg and Alfie when they've found Bert. Herbie when he's found the lad who nicked the motor, and you when you've found the whore. Right, Sid?'

Toner nodded his head, his mouth suddenly dry. He didn't relish the fact that he'd been placed on the same level as soldiers like Reg and Alfie or a labourer like Herbie. Least of all he disliked the implication that, like them, if he didn't come up with the goods he would be in the running for a display of Jack Reeder's retribution. He went out to his car, trying desperately to think of ways and means to placate Reeder. Finding the whore would be one thing, but he had a sneaking feeling it wouldn't be enough on its own.

In the office, Jack Reeder sat at his desk thinking. The time was clearly approaching when he would have to make his presence felt. People were getting sloppy, and sloppy villainy led inevitably to the nick. He glanced at the window where the light was already failing. First things first, he thought. He would have to arrange for some substitutes for Reg and Alfie. Good ones too, because after the cock-up with Gus Jacobs's body, they might very well have to be permanent.

CHAPTER SEVENTEEN

Although no one would have dared mention it, Detective-Chief Superintendent George Blackstone had one thing in common with Jack Reeder. He too was a very unhappy man.

'Bloody dwarfs,' he announced in a fierce but muted bellow.

His sergeant bobbed down behind a filing cabinet in a simulated search for a paper clip.

'They've got bodies like midgets and brains to match.'

'Yes, sir,' said the sergeant.

'You know, I know, every bloody copper in the building knows that nothing gets the villainy going like keeping 'em guessing.'

'Yes, sir.'

'And guessing they were. They didn't know we had the body, they didn't know we knew where he'd been topped and they didn't know we had a lead to who did it. Now, because some bleeding heart says we had to let that spotty kid go, everybody in Putney knows as much as we do. Worse, the whole world knows. I ask you, putting it on the television news. My God, before you know what's what they'll be shoving their cameras into the interrogation room. Well, just let them try it. Just let one of them put his nose round my door and he'll find himself filming his own bloody funeral.'

'Yes, sir,' said his sergeant. He coughed and decided the time had come to nudge his transfer along a peg or two. 'I, er, forgot to mention, sir. I saw Jack Reeder outside the Town Hall a few days ago. Looking very pleased with himself he was.' He paused, ensuring he had his superior officer's full attention. He felt, rather than saw, the gleam in Blackstone's eye, swallowed nervously and ploughed on. 'He had those two heavyweights with him, Reg and Alfie.'

'When was this, Green?' Blackstone asked with unnatural calmness.

The sergeant, whose name wasn't Green, told

him.

Blackstone stared in silence for several moments which stretched into minutes. The sergeant felt mildly elated—it seemed to be working. 'There isn't anything else, is there, Green? Any other little gem you've been keeping to yourself?'

The sergeant hesitated, then decided that to keep what he had seen at the Putney Dog Show from Blackstone might result in something a little more drastic than a simple transfer. He told the Chief Superintendent about the man with tattooed ear lobes who had stood on his foot and whose trail he had then promptly lost.

Blackstone heard him out in silence, then stood up, his bulk seeming to tower over the sergeant who, thin though he might be, was certainly no midget. The silence dragged on and the sergeant held his breath. Blackstone's expression slowly changed and, to his horror, the sergeant saw that he was actually smiling. 'Good lad, Green, good lad. I like a copper who plays things close to his chest. Shows he has his priorities right. Keep those dwarfs and midgets guessing.' The smile changed to a frown but the eyes still glimmered. 'But don't keep things from me. Remember, I'm on your side.' Blackstone pushed past the sergeant and as he did so reached out a large paw. The sergeant cringed away in fear but the Chief Superintendent's hand, clenched into a loose fist, merely pushed gently against his shoulder.

When the door had swung shut behind the big man, the sergeant tottered weakly to his chair and collapsed into it. His plans, so carefully made, had backfired with a vengeance. Now there was no hope for him. He was doomed to see out the rest of Blackstone's service with him. He raised his head, eyes dull with agony, and stared at the calendar. Still more than ten months to go. He felt pain tearing at his stomach. He'd never last out. He had to do something. Resign from the force? It was an extreme remedy—there was no other work he could do. He could try to arrange for Reeder's mob's tickle, whatever it was, to succeed. He could even try to arrange it so that whoever had topped the used car dealer from Vauxhall got away with it. The trouble with either of those schemes was that he could very easily land up in the nick himself. He thought about his ulcer. He could drink a bottle of scotch and hope to be hospitalized until the Chief's retirement day came around. The trouble was he didn't like whisky, or any other alcohol, sufficiently to get the necessary quantity into his stomach for long enough to have the desired effect.

Then came an idea. It wasn't a very good one and he didn't know how he would put it into effect, but it seemed to be his only hope. Somehow, he had to arrange it so that Blackstone's retirement was brought forward.

He sat up straighter, some of the pain easing from his stomach. It might work, just. He would have to give it a lot of very careful thought. After all, his life might very well depend on it.

Blissfully unaware of the plots and schemes being hatched by his right-hand man, Detective-Chief Superintendent George Blackstone was marching along Upper Richmond Road, his feet slamming down on the pavement. Every blow of his heel sent the fear of God into the hearts of several passers-by who knew him too well. Blackstone was on the warpath, the word went round, and it wasn't just his fellow police officers who were alarmed at the prospect. A few local villains caught the vibrations too and promptly went into hiding.

Blackstone felt he had cause for his dissatisfaction with his superiors. They had insisted on releasing the news of the dead body found in the stolen Marina. From the information spilled out by the spotty youth several things became apparent. The car, body and all, had been destined for the crusher. The two big men who had been with the car when the youth had arrived on the scene had rapidly been identified as Reg and Alfie. The problem was, the youth didn't know whether they had brought the Marina into the scrap-yard. Even the fact that Forensic claimed they could prove the body had been in the car from the moment of death didn't help. Gus Jacobs could have been killed after Reg and Alfie had left the scene and popped into the boot in time for Spotty to drive away with it. The policeman didn't believe that for a moment, but he knew any wet-behind-the-ears lawyer would soon demolish a case built on such a premise. If he could find him, Bert Dixon might help, but the chances were he wouldn't know what was in the car when he'd been given it. No, what he needed was someone close to the centre who would spill a little piece of vital evidence in exchange for a promise of a deal. That was why he'd wanted the case keeping under wraps. He had wanted time to dig, plant a few pieces of information, and get some of the local villains worried.

He shrugged his shoulders. It was too late now, word was out and he'd have to make the best of it. A smile came over his face as he thought about the effect the news broadcast might have had. Come to think of it, it might not have been such a bad thing after all. It could very well be that somebody was running scared. All he had to do was find out who. He decided to go calling on a few people, but first he needed a couple of pints. He turned into Putney High Street and stamped down towards the Red Lion.

CHAPTER EIGHTEEN

Lew Jackson wandered into the bar of the Red Lion, resplendent in an orange and brown check suit, with no real plans in mind except that the pub was the place where the Honeydripper picked up most of her customers. The bar was almost empty, so he decided he might as well start by chatting to the blonde barmaid.

'Do you always dress like that?' the girl asked before he could speak.

'Like what?'

'You know, flashy.'

Lew looked down at himself and felt affronted. 'What's wrong with the suit? It cost real money.'

'You look like my Uncle Frank.'

Lew frowned, having an uneasy feeling he didn't want to know the answer to his next question. 'Who or what is your Uncle Frank?'

'My mother's brother. He races greyhounds.'

'Does he beat them?'

'Pardon?'

'Never mind. Listen, the last time I was in here I was talking to a girl, remember?'

'That black girl?'

'Yes, she's Jamaican.'

'Legs are a bit thin,' the girl said, with a tinge of jealousy in her tone.

Lew craned over the bar and saw, from the waist down, that the girl was a little on the dumpy side. 'That's right,' he agreed.

'What about her?'

'Had you seen her before?'

'Once or twice.'

'Remember anything about the people she was with?'

The girl thought hard. 'No,' she said after a few moments. 'Can't say I can.'

Lew ordered a scotch and, as an afterthought, told the girl to give herself a drink. She poured out a discreet grapefruit juice. Something from their last conversation suddenly clicked in Lew's mind. 'What was that you were telling me? Something about your boyfriend being nicked?'

'Ex-boyfriend. Yes, pinched a car he did. Then he got himself nicked. There was a body in the boot. It was on the telly.'

'Yes, I know it was, but you told me about it before it was on the telly.'

The girl turned bright pink. 'Somebody told me,' she said.

Lew hesitated, then decided a direct approach might frighten her off. 'I'm Lew Jackson,' he said. 'I own the South Bank Jazz Club.' He grinned. 'The one you think's a bit tatty. And you're right. I'm planning on having it breezed up a bit. Changing the staff too. I could do with a bright young woman to help behind the bar.

Pay will be good and you would meet lots of interesting people. Show-business types. Fancy a change?'

The girl nodded enthusiastically. 'Yes. What did you say about the wages?'

Lew asked what she earned at the Red Lion and the girl gave him a figure he didn't believe. He added a tenner a week on top on the principle that it didn't matter as he was making the whole thing up anyway.

'When?' the girl asked.

'A couple of weeks. I'll keep in touch. What's your name?'

'Marti.'

'Eh?'

The girl's colour brightened again. 'Well, since you'll be my boss, it's really Maureen – but I prefer Marti.'

'And you've no boyfriends at the moment?'

'No.'

'The other one's definitely out of it, is he?'

'Yes. He had spots, anyway.'

'How did you meet him?'

'He worked for my Dad.'

'Keeping it in the family, eh?'

'That's what he seemed to think, but my Dad reckoned he was a bit thick. Must've been to do with what he did.'

'What's he doing now?'

'Who?'

'The ex-boyfriend.'

'I don't know.'

'He's not at work?'

'The yard's closed while my Dad's away.'

'On his holidays, is he?'

The girl's colour heightened yet again. 'Yes,' she said, and looked round as if hoping for an excuse to get away.

The bar door opened and wheezed slowly closed again. Heavy footsteps crunched up to the bar and a deep voice ordered a pint of bitter. The girl took the opportunity to scuttle away from Lew who glanced sideways at the newcomer and recognized the big policeman at once. 'Evening all,' he said.

Blackstone looked at him, his face expressionless. He ran his eyes over the suit and down to the brown and white shoes Lew had discovered underneath a pile of old magazines and paperbacks in the bottom of a cupboard in the flat. To the policeman's unsartorial eye the garb made the musician look like Rupert Bear masquerading as a bookie's runner, but he didn't say so in case it sounded like a joke. 'Come out of your rat hole, have you?' he remarked. 'Come out to contaminate a few innocent people?'

'I didn't know there were any. I thought the only difference between villains and non-villains was that you hadn't caught the others at it yet.'

Blackstone considered this remark gravely, then nodded slowly. 'Maybe you're not as stupid as you look,' he conceded. He put away in a single swallow a third of the contents of the glass the girl had stood before him, banged the glass down on to the bar and glared at her. She stood rooted to the spot while the policeman's memory circuits chuntered away. 'Maureen Dixon,' he said at last. 'You're Bert's daughter.'

The girl nodded meekly.

'I want to talk to your Dad. Where is he?'

She shook her head.

'Lost your tongue have you?' He indicated Lew with a jerk of his thumb. 'You were talking to this when I came in.'

'I was offering her a job, not playing at the Spanish Inquisition,' Lew told him.

'Are you adding to your crimes, Jackson? Interfering with a police officer in the execution of his duty? Serious business, that.'

'Since when was badgering young girls the execution of your duty?'

Blackstone sipped another third of a pint from his glass. Placing it carefully on the bar he turned towards Lew, shifting his weight on to his heels as he did so. He appeared ready to crack Lew one that would send him, or at least his head, through the plate-glass windows of the bar, but then Lew winked at him and he settled his weight again, more from shock than anything else.

'Mind your own business, Jackson,' he said, but the tone was relatively mild. He turned back

148

to the girl. 'I'll be talking to you again, miss. When your friend isn't with you.' He drained his glass and went out of the bar, his steps shaking a few flakes of loose plaster from above the door.

Lew grinned at the girl and raised his glass. 'Cheers,' he said.

'Oooh, thank you, Mr Jackson. You saved my bacon, you did.'

'Call me Lew. Anyway, I was just helping a friend,' he told her airily. He leaned forward and dropped his voice into a conspiratorial whisper. 'More important, I think I can help your Dad. He's in a spot he can't get out of on his own. He is on his own, isn't he?'

'Yes, and dead worried he is too.'

'What time do you finish here?'

'We're a bit slack so I can get off just before eleven.'

'Right, I'll meet you outside then. We can have a talk.'

'Thank you, Mr Jack ... Lew.'

'My pleasure, Marti,' Lew said, with as much smarm as he could muster. He gave her his most charming smile and went out into the street. He had gone less than thirty yards when an arm reached out from a doorway and he felt himself being heaved off the pavement.

'And what was all that about?' Blackstone breathed into his ear in a quiet rumble.

Lew straightened his jacket carefully. 'The

149

girl knows where her father is and she's more likely to tell me than you.'

Blackstone glared at him, his ridged face frowning dangerously. 'Allowing that to be true, what's it got to do with you?'

'You've got a short memory,' Lew told him. 'You're the one who came to the club, asking questions about someone who, it turns out, had been murdered. You seemed to think Honey was mixed up in it and you made it clear you weren't above thinking I might be involved. Added to which, Honey's brothers seem to think I'm responsible for her disappearance. All things considered it seemed like a good idea to find out what I could before somebody else got hurt.'

'Like who?'

'Me.'

'Gallant, that's the word for you, Jackson.' Blackstone thought for a moment. 'How did you get on to her?' His large thumb indicated the Red Lion.

'She knew about the body in the boot before it was official.'

'Ah. Clever lad.' Blackstone was silent again. 'All right, Jackson, I'm not one to complain when a citizen does his duty, even if he is a low-life like you. Talk to the girl, see what you can find out about her father. Don't keep anything to yourself, mind.'

'Don't worry, I'm not about to start playing

policeman. I just want everybody off my back.'

Blackstone picked up the word quickly. 'Everybody?'

Lew's hesitation was fleeting and he was sure the policeman wouldn't have noticed it. 'You and Honey's brothers.'

Blackstone nodded slowly. 'Okay, Jackson. Talk to the girl, see if you can find out where Bert Dixon's hiding out, then report back to me.' He fumbled in his pocket and produced a stub of pencil and a scrap of paper on which he wrote a number. 'Call me there. If I'm not in ask for Sergeant Green, he'll know where to find me.'

Lew took the paper and Blackstone marched off down the road. Lew glanced at his watch, decided he was hungry but hadn't enough time to go back to the club. Anyway, he didn't really feel like a plateful of inferior curry. He headed instead for a small Italian restaurant run by a very fat man with a thick Calabrian accent who seemed to have stepped right out of a Hollywood movie. Lew exchanged a few jokes with the owner, neither man understanding much of what the other said, but both laughing uproariously. He ate a hasty and excellent meal consisting largely of pasta and a sauce which had everything in it including, probably, a few magic spells, and felt sufficiently restored to face the task of playing detective with Bert Dixon's daughter, Marti.

Just as he reached the car park of the Red Lion the pub door opened and the blonde girl came out on to the pavement. He had raised one arm and opened his mouth to call out when he saw she wasn't alone. Two very big men were with her, one on each side, a large helping hand on each elbow. He stepped sideways, hastily taking advantage of the shadows, and waited to see what happened next. The two men helped the girl, apparently quite gently, into the back seat of a Volvo parked by the kerb, then one climbed in beside her, the other going round to get into the driving seat. For a few seconds Lew hesitated, not knowing what to do. In all the old movies he remembered, such moments were accommodated by passing taxi-cabs or even a car conveniently parked with the keys in the ignition. He looked around the car park as he heard the Volvo start up, hoping fate would grant him a happy coincidence. He had tried two car doors unavailingly when, as the Volvo moved away, he saw an elderly pedal cycle leaning up against the wall. It was beside the open door of what appeared to be the staff entrance of the pub and he could hear voices approaching along the inside passageway. Acting without further thought, he was out on the road when he heard an angry yell behind him.

He started to run with the bicycle, desperately trying to recall how he was supposed to get on the thing. Eventually he managed it, performing an ungainly sideways leap that almost carried him over to the other side of the machine. Wobbling dangerously, he began to pedal furiously in what he hoped was the same direction as that taken by the Volvo. He was relieved to see the car, or at least one of the same make and colour, a few yards further along the High Street, carefully negotiating a group of pub-leavers gathered around two young men who were in the process of beating seven bells out of one another. Lew managed to get close enough to the car to satisfy himself it was the right one, then, head down, he pedalled furiously, sweat pouring from him at the unaccustomed exertion and the mental and physical effort involved in keeping the thing balanced. He vaguely recalled reading somewhere that riding a bicycle was something you never forgot how to do. Like a lot of other theories it was in need of some overhaul.

He was beginning to think he had picked a quick way to a coronary when he glanced up from his efforts to see the Volvo had stopped opposite Flanagan's. He carried on a little further, then, as one of the men and the girl got out of the car, he hastily scrambled the machine over the pavement and took a cautious look along the road behind him. As far as he could see, the owner of the bike had given up the chase, so he pushed it carefully into a narrow gap between two shops, just in case he needed it again. He wandered casually along the pavement to the point where the man and the girl had left the car, which was still in view as it moved towards the traffic lights. Of the girl and the man there was no sign and he began looking for an entrance through which they could have gone. None of the doorways looked particularly promising until he saw one adorned with a discreet notice to the effect that it was the home of 'J.R. Enterprises'. It seemed a likely possibility so he went up to the door and, not very hopefully, tried the handle. To his surprise the door opened.

Inside was a short hallway, then stairs leading steeply upwards to a half-landing. The stairs were carpeted and, with a distinct feeling he was doing something he would, with luck, live to regret, Lew began to ease his way silently upwards.

In Jack Reeder's office, Reg was momentarily put out to find the boss had gone home. He stood hesitant, unsure what to do next but, in fact, a tiny bit relieved that Reeder wasn't there. Reeder had been quite clear in his statement that he didn't want to see his erstwhile bodyguards without Bert Dixon, and Bert Dixon was someone they hadn't got. His daughter was no substitute but would, with any amount of luck, lead them to her father. Just a few questions was all that was needed and it was

154

for the interrogation that Reg had decided to bring her there. Past experience had shown that not many sounds floated out from Reeder's office, and those few that did fell on ears which could be relied upon to go conveniently deaf at the appropriate moment. From the bottom of the stairs he heard the street door close with a bang and thought fast. He needed to decide what action he was to take before Alfie arrived – his esteem was already quite low in his direction too.

Halfway up the second part of the staircase, Lew Jackson heard the street door slam shut with a feeling approximately that of a man hearing a shilling fall into the meter just as he'd put his fingers into a broken light-bulb socket. The reason for the unexpectedly unlocked door was suddenly apparent. The driver had merely gone to park the Volvo and was now on his way upstairs. Lew thought fast. Going down was out of the question—the staircase was too narrow for any escape. Upwards was the only way, and since that too didn't leave a lot of scope he decided to try bluff, working on the simple principle that the only alternative was violence and he couldn't see that getting him very far.

On the landing were two doors, only one with a light coming from beneath it. Taking a deep breath, he knocked at the door and opened it, stepping inside before whoever was in the room could take evasive action.

It was hard to tell who was the more surprised, Reg or the girl. As for Lew, he was immediately relieved to see there was no sign of either Jack Reeder or Sid Toner. With only the hired help to deal with he stood a slight chance of getting away from there without a compound fracture of something important.

'Where's Reeder?' he asked.

'Eh?'

'He told me to be here at half-past eleven, so here I am.' Reg frowned in concentration at this unexpected turn up and at that moment Alfie arrived in the doorway behind Lew. The two big men exchanged enquiring glances and Lew took the opportunity to slide what he trusted to be a meaningful glance at the girl. 'Hello, Marti,' he said. 'You'll be late if you don't get moving.'

'Late?' Reg said.

'She's auditioning at the club in half an hour. Didn't Jack tell you?'

'Jack?'

'Reeder. He recommended her to me, said she's a good singer.'

'Singer?'

'He wants me to put her in the festival.'

'Festival?'

'Knows a thing or two about music, your boss.'

'Does he?'

'Anyway, if he isn't here maybe he'll be down

156

at the club later.' Lew turned and held out a hand to the girl. 'Come on Marti, first rule of show business, don't keep the band waiting.' He felt the girl's damp hand enter his and he pulled her towards the door and Alfie. He didn't break step as the big man cast an imploring look at his partner. Reg didn't appear to send any negative messages, so Alfie stepped aside to let Lew and the girl pass.

They were at the half-landing before the girl pulled back. Lew turned to see what the problem was.

'Are you really giving me an audition?' she asked.

Lew stared at her in astonishment. 'Are you out of your mind?'

'But you said. . . .'

'I said that to get you out of there.'

'All they were going to do was talk to me. Ask me some questions, they said.'

'About your father. And if they didn't like your answers they'd probably have ended up pulling your toe-nails out. One at a time. Now come on.'

They reached the street door without further delay or mishap. Once outside Lew headed south along the High Street, taking care he and the girl kept to the brighter-lit parts of the pavement.

He decided wherever he took her would be a risk, but his flat would be less chancy than the club or the girl's own home. They reached there in less than fifteen minutes, both out of breath, Lew sweating as well, and the girl beginning to have doubts about the entire affair. In the flat she looked around her and wrinkled her nose.

'Not very cheerful, is it? Why don't you get some pictures?'

'I have.'

The girl peered at the Savoy fliers. 'Who's Chick Webb?' she asked.

Lew shook his head sadly and decided on a quick change of subject. 'Your Dad's in trouble,' he told her. 'The police want him and Reeder's mob want him.'

'Who is this Reeder you keep talking about?'

'He's the local villain, chief of all he surveys. If it's illegal he's into it.'

'Like the Mafia?'

'He probably thinks so.'

'My Dad wouldn't be involved with anything like that.'

'Then why is he on the run?'

'He isn't on the run, he's at my sister's. . . .' The girl looked alarmed. 'Here, I'm not supposed to tell anyone where he is.'

'Why is he there?'

'Something to do with the body in the boot of that car. He reckons they're trying to pin it on him. Well, my Dad wouldn't do anything like that, my Dad wouldn't.'

'All right, Marti, I'll help him and you. You

158

needn't worry at all. Now, is this sister of yours far enough away so Reeder's boys won't find the place?'

'Yes, she lives up in Chingford.' The girl's mouth closed with a snap when she realized she'd once again said more than she was supposed to.

Lew nodded, recognized that he'd got all he could expect from her and turned to switch on the radio and open a half-empty bottle of scotch. He poured out two glasses and handed one to the girl.

'I don't drink,' she told him.

'Try it,' he said. 'It'll relax you.' He went through the door into the bedroom, turning up the volume on the radio as he did so. He telephoned the number Blackstone had given him and was put through to the big detective without delay. 'Bert Dixon is at his other daughter's house, in Chingford,' he said.

Blackstone sounded suitably surprised. 'Well done, Jackson. I owe you one just so long as you don't try to collect with interest.'

'I had to take her away from two of Reeder's heavyweights.'

'Did you now, that was brave of you.'

'Yes, wasn't it.'

'Well, maybe just a little interest,' Blackstone said, and broke the connection. Lew stared at the dead instrument, replaced it, and went out to find the girl gyrating gently to the music on the radio.

'Quite nice this,' she said holding up her empty glass.

Lew took the hint and refilled it. She downed the refill in one gulp and gyrated a shade faster. Lew sat in his solitary armchair and watched. Two refills and some even faster gyrations later the girl collapsed across his knees in a loose, soft bundle, one arm across his shoulders. He carefully removed the glass from her fingers. With both arms now free she wrapped them around his neck and placed her face where he had little choice but to kiss her.

'How old are you?' he asked.

'Old enough.'

There didn't seem to be a very satisfactory verbal response to that so, since the streets of Putney were unlikely to be very safe for the moment, he decided to help her get comfortable for the night. Part of the plan necessitated taking her into the bedroom and removing her clothes, a process with which she eagerly co-operated. Once she was safely in the bed, he went out to check the lock on the door. For safety, he pushed a chair under the handle to delay forcible entry at least until he'd had time to put his trousers on. Then he went back into the bedroom, armed with the whisky and the radio.

The girl was lying on her back, completely naked, her plump thighs spread wide to display the fact that her blondeness didn't stop with the hair on her head.

'Like?' she asked, trying hard to be coy.

'Like,' he agreed, as he sat on the bed, feeling suddenly tired.

''Nother drink.'

He poured a very small one for her and watched it disappear rapidly.

'Aren't you taking your clothes off?' she asked.

Wearily he stood up and began to undress. By the time the suit was hanging on a chair back and he was thinking about what he could do to conceal the fact that the appropriate part of his body was not reacting in a manner the girl clearly anticipated, she had helped herself to yet another drink. He knelt on the bed beside her and felt arms and legs wrap around him like a series of soft tentacles.

He was beginning to feel seriously worried by his lack of enthusiasm when he felt the girl's body begin to arch in a series of wild convulsions. He thought, with astonishment, that somehow she had managed to reach an orgasm without any outside aid but then, to his horror, realized that, far from reaching a sexual climax, she was about to be sick.

He managed to get her to the basin in the corner of the room, supporting her with both arms like a man trying to control a suddenly deflating, giant, pink balloon. When she had

161

thrown up all she had he got her back to the bed, covered her with the blanket and stood watching as she floated off into sleep. After a while he noticed that it wasn't all that warm and put his shirt and underpants back on. As an afterthought he added his socks and crawled under the edge of the blanket and lay there listening to her heavy breathing until, finally, he too drifted off into a not very restful sleep.

CHAPTER NINETEEN

Lew came out of a dream in which he was riding a bicycle along a tightrope stretched above a pit filled with trumpet-playing, bright purple crocodiles with blonde pubic hair on their heads, and heard the telephone ringing. He answered it, one hand fumbling for his trousers. It was Joe Nealis and he sounded worried.

'He's here and he's as mad as a wet hen.'

'Who is?'

'Ray Curtis.'

'Curtis?'

'Yes,' Joe yelped. 'He wants to see you and he's drinking already.'

Lew looked at his watch. 'It's nine o'clock in the morning.'

'Try telling him that.'

'Okay, I'm on my way.' He started to replace

the telephone. 'Hey, Joe.'

'What?'

'Where are you? The Town Hall or the club?'

'The club.'

'Ten minutes.'

'Faster if you can,' Joe said before hanging up.

Lew looked at the girl who was lying on her stomach, her bottom, round and inviting, uncovered by his movements. He was midly pleased to note that the sight caused a mild stir where last night there had been only flaccid flesh. Regretfully he decided duty called and finished dressing. He shook the girl by the shoulder, gently at first but harder as she refused to surface.

'Wake up, Marti. Wake up.'

'Wha. . . .'

'I have to go. Listen, stay here for another hour or so. Give me time to sort things out, so it's safe for you to be on the streets.'

'All right.'

He wasn't sure if she had understood what he was talking about, but took the chance that she was likely to go back to sleep for an hour or more anyway. He was half-way down the stairs when he remembered he hadn't washed or shaved. He thought about going back but decided to make up the deficiency at the club.

Just before he reached the club he popped into a telephone kiosk to call Blackstone and received confirmation that Bert Dixon was, in the time-honoured, press-invented phrase, helping the police with their enquiries. 'The girl's at my flat,' he told Blackstone. 'It might be an idea to keep an eye on her until Reeder's men know she can no longer be of use to them.'

'I'm not running a baby-sitting agency down here, you know,' he was told.

'Neither am I.'

'All right, I'll see she doesn't come to any harm.'

Lew thought for a moment. 'What about me?'

'What about you?'

'Jack Reeder isn't going to be very pleased with me, taking her away from his lads.'

'Knowing Jack Reeder, he isn't going to be very pleased with his lads for letting you take her away,' Blackstone remarked and hung up.

Lew knew he hadn't been given an answer to his question about his own safety but, after searching his pockets and being unable to find any more change for the telephone, decided to hope for the best.

When he reached the club there was an air of suppressed hostility coming from a small, slightly-built man who was propping up the bar, one hand wrapped loosely around a glass, the other keeping a proprietary grip on a bottle of scotch. The bottle was half empty but from the man's eyes, as he turned to watch Lew descend the last few steps, it was apparent it hadn't long been that way.

Joe Nealis appeared from the office where he'd been keeping his head down. 'Lew, this is Ray Curtis. Ray, Lew.'

The American bandleader turned his simian features towards Lew and let his eyes run from the uncombed hair, over the unwashed face and unshaven chin, down the shirt that had been slept in, past the creased orange and brown check suit to the brown and white shoes, then all the way back again. The effort and the view seemed to take a lot out of him. He gulped from the glass and promptly refilled it without seeming to need to look at what he was doing.

'Jesus Christ,' Curtis said. 'What have I let myself in for?'

Lew moved closer to the bandleader, raising an eyebrow at Joe as he did so. 'Pleased to meet you, Ray,' he said by way of greeting. He held out a hand which Curtis looked at with suspicion, then chose to ignore.

Curtis's face had a deep tan, polished by hours under the sun-lamps of the health farms where he took two vacations each year. Ostensibly the purpose of the visits was to relax and restore him to a condition in which he could withstand the rigours a life of one-night stands placed on the mind and body of a man who had been in the business since the mid-thirties. His enemies, of whom there were considerably more than there were friends, unkindly spread the

165

rumour that the visits to the farms were for nothing more than the periodical drying-out required by anyone who consumed upwards of two bottles of bourbon every day.

'He isn't very happy with the programming of the concert,' Joe said. 'He also doesn't think much of his hotel room. In addition he wants to know where he's supposed to rehearse. Added to that he thinks the acoustics at the Town Hall are lousy.' Joe's voice dropped a notch. 'If that isn't enough he drinks bourbon and we haven't any so he's making do, very reluctantly as you can see, with some of our best scotch.'

'Well, now.' Lew tried to force charm and hospitality into his voice. 'I'm sure we can sort everything out to our guest's satisfaction, can't we, Joe?'

'Are you kidding?' Joe asked, his voice still pitched low.

'*I'm* not kidding,' Curtis remarked, proving that, whatever else he might be, deaf he was not.

'Well, let's make a start,' Lew said as cheerfully as he could. 'What don't you like about the programming?'

'You've got me closing the first half of the show on Sunday night. I always close the last half.'

'You're closing the second half on Saturday night and Monday afternoon.'

'So why not Sunday.

'Because Dizzy Gillespie's closing it.'

166

'Why?'

There was a short, awkward, silence before Joe chipped in. 'Because it's Sunday.'

'What the hell has that got to do with anything?'

'The local religious community have asked us to ensure the last band of the evening doesn't make too much, er, isn't an, er, high-volume group. As Dizzy has a quartet and you have a seventeen-piece band we thought. . . .' Joe's voice trailed off as the power of invention left him.

'That's the way it is,' Lew confirmed, delighted with his partner's inspiration. 'We cannot go against the wishes of the church, now can we?'

There was silence as Curtis digested this along with another substantial intake of scotch. 'The hotel room is a mess,' he said, apparently giving in over the question of his decibel rating versus that of Dizzy Gillespie.

'It'll be changed before tonight,' Lew said hastily. With any amount of luck, he thought, by nightfall Curtis would be too drunk to notice which room he was sleeping in, let alone its condition. 'Now, rehearsals. This afternoon and tonight you can rehearse at the Town Hall. Saturday morning too if you want. Or here.'

The bandleader looked around him and shook his head slowly as if in astonishment that anyone could make such a suggestion to him. 'This stuff is no good,' he said.

For a moment Lew wasn't sure what he was talking about, then realized it was the distillers of Scotland who were under attack. 'I'll lay on a crate of bourbon by tonight,' he said. 'Two crates, in fact.'

Curtis poured another slug of the no-good spirit and stepped away from the bar. Walking up to Lew he glared at him, any fearsomeness slightly lost by the fact that the top of his head barely reached Lew's chin. 'I don't like shits,' the American said obscurely. 'If a man's a shit, he does shitty things. Once a shit, always a shit. A shit will shit on you, do shitty things. That is a fact, believe me. I speak from the experience of having dealt with shits all my life. A shit is a shit. Shit on you when you least expect it. Right?'

'Right,' said Lew.

'Right,' agreed Joe.

'Right,' Curtis repeated, and started for the stairs, then turned back to gather up the scotch bottle. 'Saturday night I go on after Scott Hamilton,' he said.

'Yes.'

'The sonofabitch is too young.' He headed for the stairs again and this time didn't turn back.

When the street door slammed Lew let out a long breath and looked at Joe. 'What was that last crack supposed to mean?'

'I expect he's feeling his age. Doesn't like to

168

think the young guys are as good as he is.'

'Better. Scott Hamilton can blow that guy off the scene any day of the week.'

'Curtis is still good, not as good as he was maybe, but good.'

'Maybe.' Lew shrugged. 'Anyway, he's gone. I need a wash and a shave.'

'You're not kidding.'

Lew looked at his partner and noted with some surprise that Joe looked much smarter than usual. 'Chris come back?' he asked.

Joe shook his head, his eyes blinking rapidly. 'No,' he said and turned away, apparently not wanting the conversation pursued.

Lew went into the office for the razor he kept there and was heading for the men's room when he remembered another of Ray Curtis's complaints. 'What was that about the acoustics at the Town Hall?'

'Acoustics?' Joe asked. 'We haven't got any acoustics in there. The last one was killed a fortnight ago.'

'My God, you have changed. Jokes at ten in the morning.'

'That's a joke?'

'Near enough.' Lew shook his head slowly. 'I hope that bastard doesn't give us any trouble.'

'He won't. He might drink and fight but he never misses a date.'

'We should've tried to get Bill Berry and the L.A. Big Band instead of Curtis.'

'No chance. For one thing they don't tour, not over here anyway. For another we could only just afford Curtis, and Berry's out of our league.'

'This year maybe. Next year. . . .' He let the words hang.

'Let's get this year's problems out of the way before we start on another batch.'

Lew grinned and nodded. He went through the door into the men's room. He was in the middle of shaving when Joe came in, more worried than ever. 'Reeder's here.'

'Here. Oh, Christ.' Lew finished off quickly, cutting his chin in the process, rinsed off the soap and dried his face before pulling up his shirt collar and looping his still-tied tie over his head.

Reeder was sitting at a table near the bandstand. At a respectful distance stood two large individuals and Lew was relieved to see they were strangers to him. 'I want a word with you, Jackson,' Reeder said.

On the principle that attack was better than defence, Lew sailed right in. 'And I want a word with you. Where did you find those two lamebrains, Reg and Alfie?'

'What?' Reeder looked surprised and annoyed at the same time.

Lew ploughed on. 'They nearly made a nasty mess of things last night,' he said. 'They were trying to kidnap a young woman.'

170

'She was. . . .'

'And not just any young woman. She was the daughter of a man in police custody.'

'Police custody?'

'The police have her father inside. Helping with their enquiries but you and I know what that means. Could've been very unpleasant if they learned your men were meddling with the daughter of someone they were thinking of charging.'

'Charging?'

Lew glanced to his right, then his left, then leaned forward. 'Accessory to murder.' With some delight he saw that Reeder had gone a touch paler. 'We don't want anything like that, do we, Mr Reeder?'

'We don't? Er, no, that's right, we don't.' Reeder stood up. Like the recently departed bandleader he barely came up to Lew's chin. 'Why are you involved?' he asked, a tinge of suspicion in his voice.

'We're partners, aren't we? This festival means a lot to me, Mr Reeder. I'm going to make both of us famous and make us a lot of money at the same time.'

Reeder nodded slowly. 'Good, good. Yes, well, thanks. I'll remember that, Lew.'

Lew smiled, relieved that he was suddenly on first-name terms with the chief villain. Reeder went up the stairs, one of his new bodyguards preceding him, the other providing rearguard

171

protection.

Reeder's batch of orders to find Bert Dixon, his spotty assistant and the Honeydripper hadn't produced very much. No Bert Dixon, due to the police having got there first. No Honeydripper because, despite all his efforts, Sid Toner hadn't been able to find any trace of her. Only Herbie had been successful. He had found the spotty youth and had taken him to the warehouse where Reeder had been able to question him. The result had been a blank. There was nothing in the non-stop stream of words from the youth to suggest he had described Reg and Alfie to the police. Scared out of his wits he might have been, but he wasn't foolish enough to admit he'd grassed. Having his hands stamped on by Reeder's highly polished size nines served only to strengthen his resolve. If that happened before he talked, what happened afterwards would be decidedly unpleasant. Eventually Reeder had let the youth go and he promptly caught the first train out of Paddington in the hope that he would be able to vanish into the landscape somewhere between London and Cardiff.

'What the bloody hell was all that about?' Joe asked as the street door closed.

'That was an exercise known as getting myself off the hook.'

'You could've fooled me. I thought it was an exercise in crawling into brown pastures.'

'He could be an unpleasant man to cross.'

'You don't have to tell me. Anyway, you're the one who borrowed money from him, not me.'

'Yes, well. Things got a bit complicated last night.'

'What things?'

'It's this business of the body in the boot.'

'Gus Jacobs.

'Yes. I helped Blackstone, the local Sherlock Holmes. Got him off my back and, indirectly it seems, let me get on the right side of Reeder.'

'If he's got a right side. Anyway, why do you want to keep in with him?'

'Because he's up to something and, like I said before, I'm not letting anybody mess up my festival.'

Nealis shrugged. 'Okay, play it both ways if you like but be careful you don't get caught in the middle.' He thought for a moment. 'Why was Blackstone on your back?'

'He's still after Honey.'

'Honey?' There was a marked change of tone in Nealis's voice but Lew didn't notice.

'Yes, but with a little bit of luck he won't need her now he's got Bert Dixon.'

'Bert Dixon? Who's he for God's sake?'

'The man I was talking about to Reeder. I found him for Blackstone and....' Lew stopped in mid-sentence. 'Look, it's all a bit complicated. I'll tell you some other time, okay?'

'Maybe you'd better,' Joe said.

Lew yawned. 'Christ, I feel rough. I think I'll go home for a bath.' He remembered the girl asleep in his bed. On second thoughts it might not be such a good idea. 'Can I go to your place? Promise I won't leave a tide-mark.'

'No,' Joe said quickly. He looked at Lew's surprised expression. 'Sorry, mate, I'm having a few problems with my landlady. Best if you don't go.'

Lew shrugged. 'Okay.' He stood up and thought about Maureen 'Marti' Dixon and the pink roundness of her body. With luck the whisky-induced illness of the previous night would have passed and she might feel like a little romp. 'I'll go home,' he said. He glanced at his watch. 'See you down at the Town Hall about three?'

'Okay, what's happening first?'

'Just a general equipment check. See everything's as it should be.' He took a deep breath. 'Forty-eight hours from now and it'll be curtain-up on Lew Jackson's first festival of jazz.'

'Good job it's not September, all the punters would be across the river watching Fulham.'

'Balls, jazz fans are too intelligent to watch Fulham.'

'All right, Chelsea, then.'

Lew grinned and climbed the stairs to the

174

street. Outside, he stood for a moment with his back to the road looking at the shabby entrance to the club. If he came out of this with any loot at all he would get new premises, he decided. Or, if that was a bit too adventurous, he'd at least get the bloody place painted.

He strolled off down the street, feeling quite pleased with life, and wasn't too badly disappointed when he found his bed empty of pink round, naked female flesh. There would be time enough for that sort of thing when the festival was over. Then, he would be a new man, one way or another. The way things had been recently, he reflected, the new man couldn't fare any worse than the old.

CHAPTER TWENTY

Lew's casual suggestion that Ray Curtis could use the Town Hall as a rehearsal room for his Chicago Big Band had proved to be something less than a good idea. If Curtis had been in an ill humour at their first meeting then he was now just short of murderous. He also looked a trifle pale and unsteady on his feet. It seemed his notorious tolerance for a substantial daily intake of bourbon did not extend to scotch. His band was made up largely of young musicians, some just out of college, others looking young enough to be still there and presumably working their vacations. By reputation, Curtis hired and fired at unnecessarily frequent intervals, letting men go just as they reached the stage where they were good enough to demand more money and, preferably, when they were within a fairly short bus ride from their home town. It was too far to pay fares from London so firing was out of the question at the moment. From the expressions on the faces of half a dozen members of the band, that was a pity. They were taking it but they weren't liking it.

Joe left the almost empty auditorium to find Lew, who was back-stage trying to get some sense out of a young sound engineer who was wearing jeans cut off at the knees and very little else.

'How is it somebody hasn't killed that bastard?' Nealis asked.

'Are we talking about any particular bastard?'

'Curtis.'

'Oh, that bastard.'

'That's the one.'

'Why, what's he up to now?'

'He's just chewed the arse off some poor slob who's been burning a hole in his lip for the last hour. He's bloody good too, poor sod, but to listen to Curtis, you'd think he was the worst trumpet player in the world.'

'Well, it's their problem,' Lew remarked unsympathetically. 'At the moment I've got

176

troubles of my own.' He turned back to the half-naked young man and began, once more, to explain to someone whose previous experience related to providing amplification systems for rock groups that the object of the exercise was to ensure that everyone heard well without being actually deafened in the process. The young man seemed unable to grasp that the acts would vary from a two-piece group or solo singers with a backing trio all the way up to a seventeen-piece band which, even unamplified, was capable of blowing the front doors off the Town Hall and half-way across the street.

The back-stage area looked unusually cluttered to Joe. Empty cases and crates filled almost every square foot of floor, leaving only narrow passages between. Lew joined him, having given up the unequal struggle, and decided to settle for unplugging any unwanted microphones himself at the appropriate moment. 'We should get rid of this lot,' Joe said. 'We'll be falling over each other as it is.'

'They can go back into the basement until they're needed.'

'I'm not built for that kind of work.'

Lew grinned. 'You're not built for any kind of work.' He looked around at the apparently deserted back-stage area. 'Where are Reeder's men? They're supposed to be doing things like that.'

'I haven't seen them.'

'They were here a few minutes ago, before I got involved with that half-dressed Marconi over there.'

'He doesn't look Italian.'

'Balls.'

'Maybe it's their coffee-break,' Joe suggested. 'Union rules.'

In the auditorium the band broke into an up-tempo version of an old Count Basie number, *Doodle Oodle*, a tune hung on to the chord sequences of *There'll be Some Changes Made*. The band sounded good, even from where Lew and Joe were standing. They moved closer to the wings of the stage, listening. Neither noticed the door to the basement open and first one, then another, finally all the labour force provided by Jack Reeder came up the stairs. Last out was Herbie, still in his boilersuit, which gave him the appearance of really belonging there. All the others looked out of place, not least Reg and Alfie who were unused to such demeaning work and who both fixed malevolent glares on the back of the unsuspecting head of the man who had helped gain their demotion to the lower ranks.

Joe was first to notice the gathering villains and nudged Lew, who ignored him. The band had reached the closing choruses with the trumpet section riding high over a tightly riffing saxophone section. Then the drummer took a four-bar break which gave everyone time to take in all the breath they needed for a devastating ride-out with the young, much-maligned trumpet player finding a searing Maynard Ferguson-like super C.

'Jesus Christ,' Lew whispered to Joe in the silence which followed. 'If they play half as well as that on Saturday night they'll blow the fucking roof off.'

'The boys are back,' Joe told him. 'Who's going to ask them to kindly shift the rubbish into the basement?'

'I will,' Lew said, and turned to meet the concentrated stares of Reg and Alfie. 'On second thoughts, I'd better see if our big bad bandleader needs another shot of scotch.' Before Joe could quibble with this sudden change in plan Lew ducked beneath some dangling wires the electronic expert hadn't managed to find a home for and went across the stage. He was met half-way by the band, who were heading for the dressing-room. He passed the young trumpet player who was massaging his top lip, an expression of acute hostility on his face.

'Bloody marvellous,' Lew said to him.

'Beats working for a living,' the young man mumbled through his hand.

'Be back here at two-thirty, sharp,' yelled Ray Curtis at the backs of his retreating musicians.

'Once a shit,' the trumpet player remarked to Lew as he continued on his way.

Lew reached Curtis and took a deep breath

179

before speaking. 'Band sounded fine,' he said.

'Bunch of Goddam school-kids. Have to wipe their fucking asses for them.'

'Talented, though.'

Curtis shrugged, then seemed to recognize who was talking to him. 'Hey, that scotch you gave me. . . .'

'Yes, sorry about that. I'll get the bourbon sent. . . .'

'No, the hell with that. I like that scotch. Got a kick to it. I'll have another bottle or two.'

'On its way,' Lew told him, and waited in case there was anything else, but Curtis seemed to have forgotten his complaints of the previous day. 'You're recording a programme for BBC television tonight,' Lew said.

'That's right. Lousy pay but it'll keep the guys in the band from going on the town and dissipating their fucking selves.'

'Right,' Lew said trying to keep his eyebrows in check.

'Just who the hell is this guy Parkinson?' Curtis asked.

'Don't worry about him,' Lew said. 'Just be yourself and he'll love it. Don't let him kid you he knows anything about jazz. He once shook hands with Duke Ellington and he's never been the same since.' He thought for a moment. 'What time does the recording start?'

'Eight.'

Lew nodded. 'I'll see you get your scotch

before then.'

'Christ, I hope you will, that's seven hours away.'

'Oh, you'll have some well before then,' Lew said hastily. 'I meant there's something special I want you to try.'

'Great.' Curtis grinned at him. 'You're not the shit I took you to be,' he remarked.

'That's a relief,' Lew said. He wandered away, resisting an impulse to belt the American in the mouth on the principle that no musician ever hits another where he earns his living. He went out through the front doors of the Town Hall, intent on finding somewhere that could sell him two or three bottles of Chivas Regal. With any luck he would be able completely to sabotage the recording of the Michael Parkinson Show, thus gaining some small measure of revenge for never having been invited on it himself.

He was half-way down the steps of the Town Hall when he was confronted by a small, rabbity man whom he didn't at first recognize. The little man was well into his second garbled sentence before Lew tuned in properly and simultaneously identified him as the council official who had agreed so readily to the hiring of the hall.

'. . . four hundred signatures means a lot of dissatisfied voters,' the man was saying.

'A petition?'

The little man tried to glare but failed because rabbits don't have the capacity. 'What have I been saying? A petition to the council demanding the cancellation of the festival.'

'This festival?'

'Of course, this festival,' the little man yelped.

'Why?'

'It's the noise abatement people. They've been round this morning with their decibel counters. They didn't look very pleased.'

'I'll bet they weren't,' Lew said. If anyone had pointed such a device at the Town Hall during the last chorus of *Doodle Oodle* he was very probably still looking for pieces of the machine along the railway embankment.

'It's no laughing matter.'

Lew frowned, suddenly aware that it wasn't. 'I'll have a word with the sound engineers. They were testing the equipment this morning. It'll be nothing like as loud during the actual performances.'

The little man looked a shade happier. 'That's all right then.' He sniffed, his top lip jumping up to reveal teeth more than capable of savaging a careless carrot. 'I hope Mr Reeder appreciates what I'm doing for him,' he added, rubbing his fingers together. He turned and darted away, leaving Lew looked slightly startled. It took him a few moments to work out that the rubbing motion had been intended as the time-honoured sign for dropsy. That accounted for the rapidity with which he'd been able to book the hall. Reeder had greased the wheels before he got there. He stood on the steps, thinking about his comments to Joe that he wouldn't let Reeder mess up the festival. He knew now that his words had a hollow ring to them. Without Reeder the festival would have been a non-starter, even at this late stage, without him it would fizzle into nothingness faster than snow on a whore's hip. He knew, when he allowed himself to think about it, that he was being used, but the closer the start of the festival got the less he liked to think about it. Just in case he discovered something he didn't want to know.

He descended two more steps and was greeted by yet another man whom he didn't immediately recognize. It was his bank manager, guardian of his own and the club's overdraft. He managed a smile.

'Things seem to be on the up and up, Mr Jackson,' the man said, indicating the posters around the doors of the Town Hall. 'Perhaps some of the activity will find its way into the account in due course.'

Lew realized that his bank manager was very probably mystified over the financial implications of the fact that he was apparently promoting an obviously expensive affair from a standpoint of no money at all. 'I'm just a front man,' he said weakly.

'Even front men get paid,' the bank manager pointed out reasonably.

'I have every hope of things sorting themselves out soon,' Lew said piously, with palpable insincerity.

'I am pleased to hear it.' The bank manager smiled with an equal lack of sincerity and moved on, clearly not believing a word of it. Lew watched him go in through the doors of the bank and tried yet again to get off the Town Hall steps.

'Lew.'

'Oh, Christ,' he said and turned to see Nealis coming down towards him. 'What now?'

'My word, aren't we aggressive. What did our friendly bank manager want? Apart from a reduction in the overdraft?'

'Apart from that, nothing.'

'It figures. Look, mate, you'd better have a word with your buddy-buddy, Jack Reeder.'

'What about?'

'All the stuff in the back-stage area.'

'I thought it was going in the basement?'

'Seems not. Something about a fire hazard.'

'Okay, I'll see if something can be done. Now, for Christ's sake, can I go and buy a bottle of scotch?'

'That bad?'

'It's for a friend.'

'I'll bet.'

As Lew disappeared in the direction of the

nearest off-licence Joe started back up the steps, then changed his mind and turned to head back towards the club to see how the musicians rehearsing there were getting along.

At the doors of the Town Hall two pairs of eyes watched the thin figure go. Reg looked at Alfie and nodded. 'Let's get the stuff shifted,' he said, and closed the doors tightly against any prying eyes.

There was only one pair of eyes on them, not particularly prying ones at that. A tall, miserable-looking police sergeant unglued himself from a doorway opposite and shambled over towards the Town Hall. Half-way there he changed his mind and decided to go into the bank next door to cash a cheque in the hope that it wouldn't bounce, since his month's pay wouldn't be in the account for another couple of days. Again he hesitated, then decided to go into the bank at the other side of the Town Hall in the faint hope that, since it wasn't his branch, it might take a little longer to filter through to his account. That done he planned on having a look at what Reg and Alfie were up to. It couldn't be much – even they couldn't find anything worth stealing in Putney Town Hall.

CHAPTER TWENTY-ONE

'Hey, lover, c'mon down here.'

At the shriek of delight from the small, extremely fat singer, Detective-Chief Superintendent Blackstone made a desperate bid to turn and go back up the stairs and out of the club. He stumbled and slipped and felt a small, pudgy hand grip his ankle with surprising strength. Out of nothing more than self-defence, he backed down the stairs, turning to confront Big Mama Richards who, forced to release his ankle, transferred her grasp to his wrist where she clung on with equal tenacity.

The singer had been running through her programme for the Saturday evening concert with Sammy Allon, whom Lew had persuaded to take on the unenviable task of leading the quartet which was to accompany the unpredictable, temperamental singer. Surprisingly enough things had gone well, Sammy's obvious competence and efficiency proving an agreeable surprise for Big Mama. Now, satisfied with the prospects for her first British concert appearance, she had been sitting at a table near the stairs listening to Clark Terry who, like her, was appearing with musicians he'd never met before. He wasn't having such an easy time of it and his face, usually friendly and smiling, was beginning to look slightly edgy.

'Kindly let go of my arm,' Blackstone rumbled.

'Hey, lover, what's the matter? You come and sit here and tell me all about yourself.' The little woman pulled and Blackstone, unprepared, sat down to avoid the even greater indignity of falling into her lap.

'Madam, I am a police officer,' Blackstone began threateningly.

'Say, now that's what Lew Jackson told me. You know, I wasn't sure if he was fooling or not but if you say so, then I believe it. You don't look like a man who would lie to a helpless little lady like me.'

Blackstone made a move to stand but Big Mama shot out a restraining hand which ended up high on his leg. He froze to the spot. 'I have business with Mr Jackson and his partner,' he said.

'Well, they ain't here. So until they arrive, you and me can just sit and visit.' She leaned forward, her smile widening to show small, even, very white teeth. 'Do you carry a gun?'

'No.'

'Hey, that's what I heard. You English policemen must be very brave.'

'We seldom find it necessary.'

'I bet you don't.' She squeezed his thigh, making him wince more in embarrassment than pain. 'What about a nightstick? You've got one of those, I bet.'

'I beg your pardon, madam?' Blackstone said, his dignity affronted, unhappily aware of the musicians on the bandstand who were delightedly listening, Clark Terry's smile at last returning.

'You, know, your billyclub.'

Blackstone went puce, then realized what she was talking about. 'You mean, my truncheon.'

Muffled sounds of hysteria came from the bandstand and Blackstone turned a gleaming eye on them before looking back to find Big Mama beginning to look at him with slightly different eyes. He swallowed, not happy with this new, as yet unfathomed, expression.

'How old are you?' she asked.

Taken aback at the unexpected question, Blackstone answered without thinking.

'You don't look fifty-five,' Big Mama said, musingly. 'You look in pretty good shape to me. Married?'

'My personal affairs are no business of yours, madam.'

'Hey, lover, what' all this "madam" business? You make me sound like a whorehouse-keeper. Call me Ruby.'

'Ruby?'

'You didn't think I was christened Big Mama, did you?'

'I never gave the matter any thought,'

188

Blackstone said, beginning to take command and relieved to hear the musicians had begun talking amongst themselves, apparently about their music.

'Now, that isn't friendly. You and me should have a little talk. You're not married, are you?'

He started to shake his head before he could stop himself, then, realizing he wasn't going to win, acknowledged defeat as gracefully as he knew how. 'I am not married.'

'Your wife dead?'

'Divorced.'

'Didn't like being married to a copper, eh?'

'That's right.'

'Some women don't know a good bet when they see one,' she said, unexpectedly. 'Right, how long before they spring you?'

'I beg your pardon?'

'Hey, now, don't go stiffening up on me again.' She winked lewdly. 'At least, not that way. When do you retire?'

'Madam, I. . . .'

'Ah, c'mon Blackie. When do you retire?'

'Ten months from now.'

'Is that right?' Big Mama stared at him, her black face a round, benign, impenetrable mask. She stood up suddenly and Blackstone took the opportunity to stand up also. Her head came about half-way up his chest, but that didn't prevent him having a slight feeling of inferiority. She jerked a thumb and turned

189

towards the bar. 'C'mon, you and me have something to do.' She marched behind the bar, picked up a bottle and Blackstone, his need for a drink overcoming his natural caution, followed. The singer picked up a bottle of gin, turned and was out from behind the bar before he could take evasive action. Big Mama's free hand took his arm again and he felt himself being propelled into the tiny office behind the bar. She managed to get them both inside and close the door without actually bursting out the walls of the place although the tiny desk, which had served Lew and Joe valiantly for many years, began to creak alarmingly as Blackstone's weight was pressed against it.

Big Mama leaned forward, her large, rounded breasts pressing against a point somewhere around the policeman's waistline in a manner he found most alarming. 'There's a few tests you have to pass,' she told him enigmatically.

'Tests?'

She unscrewed the cap from the gin bottle and swallowed about a quarter of it, then passed it to him. The relief at getting some sort of support, moral or otherwise, was too much temptation and Blackstone put away, in one gargantuan swallow, a percentage of the remaining contents that left the black singer wide-eyed in amazement. 'Well, that's one test passed,' she told him.

He looked at her blankly.

'Now for the other one.' She reached out and snapped off the light switch. The basement room which housed the club was usually quite dark even at mid-day and the poky office was frequently darker still. In the sudden darkness Blackstone felt a plump hand reach out and seize his trousers in a significant area. He gave a strangled yelp that mixed surprise, alarm and outrage and tried to escape backwards. There was nowhere to go and the desk began to buckle. Big Mama's flashing fingers found the top of his zip and whipped it downwards with a practised sweep. He felt her other hand dart inside and fumble around and, despite his attempts to maintain a suitably policeman-like decorum, he began to react in a way that hadn't happened for much longer than he cared to think about.

'Jesus Christ, lover, if it's like this when you ain't ready, you might be too big for little old me when you are.' Big Mama's comment was followed by her shriek of laughter which reverberated in the enclosed space and clearly indicated she didn't expect it to be taken seriously.

Before the big policeman could find a satisfactory answer the door to the office opened and Joe Nealis's angular shape appeared in the opening. 'What the hell is ... oops, sorry,' he amended as his eyes made out the shapes.

Big Mama switched on the light and turned to

grin at him. 'Don't worry, lover,' she told him. 'We're just visiting.' She sailed past Joe who watched her go, then turned and for the first time recognized the policeman. He stared in disbelief at Blackstone, his eyes eventually settling on the big man's groin where the combination of unzipped trousers and semi-aroused policeman's truncheon were proving incompatible. Blackstone turned away hastily and fumbled at his clothing. When he turned back his face was a bright, mottled red and there was a gleam in his eyes which bore signs of warning for anyone who might get in his way. At that moment, only Joe Nealis was in his way.

'I want to talk to you,' Blackstone said.

'Oh?'

'Yes, oh. You have a flat in Fawe Park Road.'

'That's right,' Joe said cautiously.

'We have been there, this morning.'

'You've what?'

'Searched it.'

'But, you're not supposed to do. . . .'

'Search warrants, is that what you're thinking about?' Blackstone reached into an inside pocket and produced two folded pieces of paper. 'One for your flat and one for Jackson's.'

'You've no right,' Joe said weakly.

'No right? I have every right. You and Jackson were the last people to see a young woman who has disappeared. A young woman who I believe may be able to help me in my

192

enquiries. Every right, sonny. Every right.'

'But I should have been there.'

'To do what? Hide the evidence? Too late. I've found it.'

'Evidence of what?' It was Lew's voice, coming from behind Joe.

Blackstone pushed his way out of the office and took up a position where he had control over access to the staircase. 'Now you're both here, we can get on,' he said. 'Evidence that a woman has been in your flat during the past few days. Yours too,' he said to Lew.

'That was Bert Dixon's daughter. I told you about her.'

'So you did, but there's nothing to say I believe you, is there?' He turned away from Lew, clearly not interested in pursuing the matter of the girl who had spent the night in his flat. He glared at Joe. 'Your neighbours and your landlady were very forthcoming. Gave me a very good description of the girl. Seems they don't approve of such goings on—you, a white man, fornicating with this black whore.'

'Here, what're you saying?' The angry voice of Big Mama Richards cut in and Blackstone turned to meet the attack. 'What in hell's wrong with a black girl making love to a white man, or vice versa? Eh?'

Blackstone shook his head from side to side. 'Wrong? Nothing's wrong. It's not against the law. . . .'

'I'm not talking about the law, lover, I'm talking about you. Do you think it's wrong?'

Blackstone's face creased in deep-set lines. 'I don't know, I've never even thought about it. Good God, woman, what does it matter what colour they are?'

'That's what I say, lover. So what were you meaning? Saying all those things about black whores and fornicating.'

'She *is* a black whore, for God's sake,' Blackstone bellowed. He saw the gleam in Big Mama's eye. 'I mean she's a whore, that's how she lives. And she's black. That's all.' He cast a despairing look at Lew, who nodded amiably at Big Mama.

'It's right,' he said. 'Honey's a whore and she comes from Jamaica.' He turned to Joe. 'That is, if we're talking about Honey.'

'We are,' Blackstone said.

Lew didn't take his eyes off Joe, who nodded slowly. 'Yes, she's been staying with me,' he admitted.

'And where is she now?' Blackstone asked.

Joe frowned. 'Where? She's still there.'

'No she isn't.'

'But. . . .'

'Shut up, Joe,' Lew cut in.

'Keep out of this, Jackson,' Blackstone threatened.

'Balls.'

'Now listen to me, Jackson. Your partner has

been sheltering someone involved in a murder.'

'That isn't so,' Joe said angrily. 'She had nothing to do with it.'

'How do you know?'

'She told me.'

'And you believe her, do you? A bla. . . .' He broke off and cast an apologetic glance at Big Mama before continuing. 'You'd believe a whore?'

'Why not, lover?' the little woman put in. 'There were whores before there were policemen.'

'That has nothing to do with it. The woman is constantly associating with criminals. She probably has one poncing for her.'

'No she hasn't,' Joe and Lew said together.

'It's immaterial,' Blackstone said, his colour heightening. 'In any case, I don't have to justify my actions to you. I must ask you to accompany me. . . .'

'Oh, bloody hell,' Lew said. 'Can't this wait? We have a festival starting tomorrow afternoon at three o'clock. I need Joe.'

'What do I care? You know what I think about you and your bloody festival. I've told you before, as far as I'm concerned all jazz musicians should be. . . .' His voice trailed off and he cast an alarmed glance at Big Mama who was moving closer to him, a decidedly unfriendly look in her eye. 'Now, stay where you are,' he said. 'This is police business.' His voice had taken on a different note and Big Mama hesitated.

'I think you'd best keep out of it,' Lew said quietly. He glanced at Joe. 'Look, why not go with Blackstone voluntarily? I'll call a lawyer and have him down at the station before you get there.' He looked at Blackstone. 'I take it you have no objections?'

Blackstone shook his head. 'I'm all for the quiet life,' he said, without much conviction.

Joe shrugged his shoulders. 'Okay. What have I got to lose? All I own is a half share in this rat-trap and a set of drums that need new heads anyway.'

Lew stood watching his partner walk towards the stairs with Blackstone. It was the policeman who looked back. 'I'll see you later,' he said. It wasn't until the street door closed behind them that Lew realized he had been talking to Big Mama Richards, not him.

'You've made a hit there,' he said.

The fat little woman frowned. 'I'm not sure I want that kind of friend,' she said. 'Pity, after he'd passed the first two tests.'

Before Lew could ask her what she was talking about she had joined the musicians on the bandstand who were packing up their instruments now there was no excitement to watch.

Lew went into the office and, with some difficulty, opened the desk drawer which was bent where Blackstone had sat on it. He found an ancient address book and looked up the number of a solicitor who played better than average trombone with an amateur band out in Pinner. In the club's early days he had spent much of his free time from Guildford Law College there. As Lew dialled the number he found himself wondering how much of Blackstone's suspicions about Joe were justified. By the time the solicitor answered his call his thinking had progressed far enough for him to feel heartily ashamed of himself.

He was also ashamed of the fact that, almost before he had replaced the receiver, his mind was floating off Joe and his predicament and was concerning itself once more with the festival.

CHAPTER TWENTY-TWO

'You should have told me,' Lew said.

'Why?'

Lew and Joe were in Lew's elderly Granada travelling along Upper Richmond Road, the police station thankfully behind them, the traffic lights on the junction with the High Street preventing them from making a turn which would take them down towards the Town Hall. Joe's incarceration had been brief and it was still on the right side of midnight. The combined efforts of Blackstone and his sergeant hadn't been able to find anything which pointed to Joe having done anything illegal. True, he hadn't told the police he knew where Honey had been during the first few days after her 'disappearance', but as she herself hadn't been wanted for anything other than questioning the best the law could have mustered was a charge of obstruction. Blackstone clearly couldn't be bothered with that and had let Joe go.

'Blackstone didn't seem all that interested, anyway,' Joe said, more to break the silence than for any other reason.

'He's not an idiot, even if he does behave like one occasionally. He must know Honey can't tell him much and you certainly can't.'

'Honey doesn't know anything about Jacobs. We talked about it.'

'What did happen between you two?' Lew asked.

Joe hesitated, then shrugged his shoulders. 'The day we had the rehearsal, I went out of the club just after Honey. She was still in the street, so we walked along together. She was worrying over whether her voice was good enough or not. She was taking the whole thing much more seriously than you were, so I tried to reassure her that there really was something and it just needed work.'

'So?'

'So, we ended up going back to my place. After . . . well, later on, I offered to coach her.'

'Coach her?' Lew said, his voice strangling on the words.

Joe glared at him. 'Why not? Just because I can't sing worth a light doesn't mean I don't know the rights and wrongs of it. Christ, I've been listening to you airing your tonsils for the last thirty years.'

'Okay, okay. Calm down.' Lew eased the car forward and turned into the High Street. 'So you offered to coach her, in return for suitable favours, I presume?'

'Don't be so fucking snide,' Joe said, his tone angry and something of a shock to Lew, who now realized that his partner was taking the whole thing to heart.

'Why didn't you say something? Why keep it to yourself?'

'Because all I would have got from you were the smart cracks I'm getting now. Then, later, when we heard about the murder, we decided it would be best to keep her out of the way of the police. At least until things settled down a bit.'

'So, where is she now?'

'I don't know. Christ, I've been telling Blackstone that all evening.'

'That was true?'

'Yes. She was there when I came out this morning.'

'What about the blood?' Lew asked.

Nealis was silent. That worried him. The police search of his flat had revealed fresh bloodstains on a towel thrown on top of the overflowing waste-bin in the kitchen. It hadn't been there when he went out and the police assumption that the blood was Honey's seemed reasonable. 'It's possible the police weren't the only ones who wanted to talk to Honey,' he said.

Lew glance at him. 'Meaning?'

'If the police thought she might know something about Jacobs then maybe whoever killed him thought the same.'

Both were silent again, only this time it wasn't the silence of antagonism. Lew was the first to break it. 'I think we'd better get some help.'

'Like who, for instance?'

'Like Honey's brothers, for instance. They were pretty hot to do me a serious mischief. If they hear a whisper about this they'll be after you. So, we see them first, tell them everything and enlist them on our side. We might get a lead to where she is before anyone else catches up with her.'

'Always assuming they haven't already.'

Lew slowed and negotiated a double-parked van before turning into the street where the Honeydripper's family home was situated. Twenty minutes later Lew, Joe, Winston, Dwight and a third brother, Everton, were in the Granada with Lew taking directions from Dwight. One at a time the three West Indians were dropped off at places where they could begin knocking on doors and asking questions of people who might know something and could also, if the need arose, be called upon for aid.

By the time Joe and Lew were alone in the car once more both felt marginally more cheerful at the prospects before them. Glancing at his watch, Lew saw it was past two o'clock and turned the Granada towards the Town Hall.

'Where are we going now?' Joe asked.

'I thought I'd have a last look at the hall, make sure everything's okay.'

'If it isn't, it's too late to do anything about it now.'

Lew parked outside the rear door of the hall and opened up with a key he had tucked carefully away in his fat, paper-filled wallet. There were a couple of security lights burning back-stage and in the glow from them it was immediately apparent that the place had been tidied up.

'At least they've got the crates down into the cellar,' Joe said.

'See, I told you not to worry.'

'Well, thanks anyway for seeing Reeder.'

'I didn't, I forgot, I was too busy getting some Chivas Regal for Ray Curtis. Speaking of which, I wonder if he managed to screw up Parkinson's programme.'

'What are you talking about?'

Lew grinned, 'Nothing,' he said.

'Well, if you didn't arrange for the stuff to be shifted, who did?'

'They must have done it on their own.'

'Ah, well, it's done anyway.' Joe turned at a sudden sound. 'What was that?'

'What?'

'I thought ... Christ, who are you?'

A large, shadowy shape loomed out of a dark corner behind the lighting console. 'Who wants to know?' a voice asked.

'Are you one of Reeder's men?'

'I work for Mr Reeder,' the shape said. 'Now, who are you?'

'I'm Lew Jackson and this is Joe Nealis.'

'Yes, well, nobody said anything about people coming back here tonight so maybe you'd better hop it.'

'Hop it? Christ, it's my bloody festival,' Lew said indignantly.

'I said, hop it,' the voice threatened.

'Come on, Lew. It's time you got some sleep anyway. You've got a busy day tomorrow.'

'Bloody nerve,' Lew muttered, but followed Joe as he led the way out through the door into the alleyway.

'Funny smell in there,' Joe remarked.

'I didn't notice.'

'Yes, like you get when you pass a house that's being knocked down. You know, all brick and plaster dust and the smell of burning. And vinegar.'

'Vinegar?'

Joe shrugged. 'Maybe it was Curtis's lead

202

trumpet player, trying to harden his lip.'

'Come on, let's go home.'

They got into the Granada and drove out into the main street, completely traffic-free at that time of the morning. As they went across the front of the Town Hall, Joe remembered the meeting with the bank manager. 'Will we be able to reduce our overdraft when this lot's over?' he asked.

Lew shrugged. 'Maybe, maybe not. Who can tell?'

'That's an answer?'

'It'll have to do. We're about two-thirds booked for Saturday and Sunday afternoon. Saturday night is almost sold out. Sunday night and Monday afternoon aren't too good but with luck they'll pick up when word gets around.' He slowed the car. 'Do you want to kip at my place?'

Joe shook his head. 'Better not. Honey might try to get in touch with me. I'll go home.'

Lew accelerated before going back to the matter of their finances. 'So, if all goes reasonably well with late bookings, then by the time we've squared up with Reeder and his merry band we should be able to pay the rent, clear the overdraft and still have enough left over to give the club a lick of paint. If we manage to sell out for the last three concerts then we should be better off than we've been for years.'

'That won't take much, I've been scratching around for pennies since we came off the road.'

'We were scratching around then.'

'Who's arguing?'

Lew turned on to Putney Bridge Road and headed for Joe's flat. He didn't pursue the matter. Joe was becoming a bit too prickly for casual conversation.

CHAPTER TWENTY-THREE

Herbie wiped his fingers on his boiler suit, the action leaving a trail of greasy marks. He looked at the others who were finishing off their fish and chips and carrying out similar cleansing actions to their grease-laden fingers.

'Not only is your beer rotten, you don't know how to fry fish and chips,' the Manchester-based peterman remarked disagreeably.

'What's wrong with it?'

'One, too much batter. Two, too little fish. Three, this lot hasn't seen the sea for weeks. Four. ...'

'Eh, man, whier doanh ye giahrahst?' the man with the tattooed ear lobes rumbled.

The man from Manchester lapsed into discontented silence, earning mild approbation from the Londoners present at the ease with which he appeared to understand the big

204

Geordie's words.

They were assembled in the basement of the Town Hall, six out-of-town specialists together with Herbie, Reg and Alfie and three other disgruntled members of Jack Reeder's team of labourers. None of the locals was very happy at the prospect of being cooped up in the basement for the next three days. Especially as there were more important pursuits to follow on the surface, what with dog-track meetings and Fulham being at home twice over the holiday weekend.

From the door at the top of the steps which led from the cellar came a furtive tap, then a pause, another tap, another pause, a final tap.

'Knock three times and ask for Nellie,' someone muttered. Nobody laughed.

Herbie went up to unlock the door and admit Sid Toner who came down the steps, his nose wrinkling at the strong smell of vinegar. 'Everything okay?' he asked.

'Apart from the food,' the Mancunian told him.

'It'll do,' the Welshman put in.

'Whiffs a bit,' Sid remarked.

'We'll put the extraction fan on later, when there's a bit of noise upstairs.'

'Another lot will be rehearsing up there tonight,' Sid told them. 'That should be enough to let you get started on the first opening.' He glanced at the man from Manchester, uncertain whether he or the Welshman was the appointed spokesman for the specialists. 'Which way are you going first?'

'Both ways at once,' the Welshman said.

'Both? Won't that make a lot of noise?'

'Doahn ye worrah, ma bonny lad,' the Geordie said, and much to his surprise Sid understood him. It didn't stop him worrying, though. Something of his expression must have relayed itself to the assembly and he was irritated to see one or two grins pass round.

'There are five explosions—it's asking a lot for them all to be covered by the sound from the hall,' Toner said.

'Only two tonight, just so we can break out of here and take all the gear through into the chambers on either side,' the Welshman told him. 'We save the next three charges for Saturday afternoon.' He consulted a much-fingered handbill advertising the concerts. 'The last band on Saturday afternoon is Art Blakeys Jazz Messengers. According to our calculations they'll make enough noise to cover what we're doing down here.'

'Yeah, Herbie here went up to Ronnie Scott's club last night and took a decibel reading. Nearly blew the needle off the fucking scale,' his Manchester colleague put in.

'Then, on Saturday night, we'll have the next big bang when Geordie here blows both bank vaults.' Again a consultation with Lew's neatly printed handbill. 'Ray Curtis and the Chicago Big Band are on last. They were in here this morning. They're loud as well. Nearly perforated my eardrums, they did. That just leaves the jeweller's vault. Geordie's keeping that for Sunday afternoon when Art Blakey's on again.'

'What about all the safes?'

'We're not using explosive for them,' someone put in scornfully. 'What the fucking hell do you think we're here for?'

Sid nodded hastily. There was nothing to be gained by antagonizing anyone at this late stage in the proceedings. 'Okay,' he said. 'I can see you've got everything under control. Right, I'll hop it, then. I won't be back, unless you need me, until Saturday night. If you need anything before then, send Herbie here. Remember, apart from him, nobody goes outside.'

There was a grumbled chorus of groaning assent and he turned to go back up the steps, preceded by Herbie who unlocked and opened the door after first exchanging a complicated series of tapping signals with someone on the other side.

In the area behind the stage Sid Toner sniffed the dusty air as if it was an ocean breeze. 'Like a bloody whore's G-string down there,' he remarked to the labourer propping up the wall beside the door. The man nodded respectfully. 'Okay, I'm off,' Sid went on. 'Remember, nobody in, apart from me or Mr Reeder or anyone with orders from us. And nobody out except Herbie.' The man nodded his understanding of his orders.

Toner walked towards the street door kicking aside a few wood shavings, originally from the packing cases which had cluttered up the area a few hours earlier to Joe Nealis's great concern, and which were now all that remained of them.

As he drove away from the back of the Town Hall in his wife's anonymous Mini, Toner couldn't resist a last look at the frontage. He drove out on to the main road and across the front of the building. There they stood; the Town Hall, imposing with its wide steps and fluted columns supporting an imitation Grecian arch much loved by generations of passing pigeons and now bedecked with posters advertising the coming weekend's festival. On one side of the town hall stood a branch of Barclay's Bank, its doors just being closed as the last customer came out. On the other side of the Town Hall stood a branch of Lloyd's Bank, its black horse sign making it look for all the world like an upper-class pub. Then, beyond Lloyd's, the jewellers, biggest in South London, or so their advertising claimed.

It had all been very handy, he thought, finding out about the interconnecting cellar system which had been carefully bricked up during conversions twenty-five years ago and now forgotten by everyone except one retired council bricklayer who, in all innocence, had passed the word to Toner's contact, the man in the dark blue Rolls-Royce. It had been fortunate that, shortly afterwards, the old man had gone to the big building site in the sky. It had meant one less mouth to close. Now it was all set. By tonight, as he'd just been informed, they'd be into the adjoining cellars, bricked up at both ends but easy prey to the big Geordie's explosive charges. By tea-time on Saturday they'd be into the basement of both banks and the jewellers and on Saturday night the vaults and safes would be open and they'd be gathering up cash and jewels in quantities that made his mouth water.

He frowned suddenly. Getting the stuff away wasn't really a problem—they had all Sunday night and all day Monday to do it—but if he'd thought about it earlier they could have used those packing cases to shift the loot. Pity he hadn't thought of that when Reg and Alfie had come along, worrying him about the packing cases and what to do with them. He'd told them to take the cases somewhere and dump them. The local inhabitants, ever eager for anything with which to board up broken windows or repair doors or furniture or simply store away as fuel for when winter came, would soon make off with a pile of wooden crates, however big it was.

It never occurred to him for one moment that

Reg and Alfie, fresh from their triumphant cocking-up of the killing of Gus Jacobs, could have made a mess of such a simple task.

Back at the Town Hall, in the basement beneath the stage, Herbie crawled out through a hole the big Geordie had blown in the wall of the passageway leading towards the basements of Lloyd's Bank and the jewellers. He removed the paint-sprayer's mask he had used to keep dust from his lungs.

'Well?' the big Geordie asked.

'Lovely job, mate. Lovely.'

The Welshman turned to Reeder's labourers. 'Right, lads, start taking the stuff through. Explosives up against the far wall, then cutting gear ten feet away. Leave the electronic gear in here until we've had the next blow. Delicate stuff it is.'

'What about the sleeping bags?' Herbie asked. 'Where are we bedding down?'

'Smells in here,' the Welshman commented. 'I'll kip in the passageway.'

'Me too,' the man from Manchester said. He looked at the Londoners, who had begun to move the explosives, their faces clearly indicating that moving the stuff was bad enough, but sleeping with it was out of the question.

Reg put it into words for them. 'We'll stay in here.'

'Suit yourself. Those fish and chip wrappers

still stink.'

An hour later they were all settled down in their sleeping bags. The two electronics experts were in the passageway behind Lloyd's with one of the petermen. The screwsman and the other two petermen, including the big Geordie, were at the other side of the Town Hall basement, in the passageway leading down to Barclay's Bank. All six Londoners were in the main basement area. It was some time before they all slept, and up above them the man who had persuaded Joe and Lew to leave didn't sleep at all. He wasn't about to put a foot wrong with Mr Reeder, who hadn't been in a very good humour lately and could be very aggressive at such times.

Jack Reeder himself was also wide awake in his home in Coombe Lane. After some considerable effort he had managed to compile a list of all the dark blue Rolls-Royces registered in the London area, and from them had made up a short list of three which had digits similar to those supplied by Gus Jacobs on the day he had proved his usefulness too satisfactorily for his own good. The owners of the three cars seemed harmless enough and, although one of them had been a bit of a surprise, none belonged to anyone with connections with any rival gang. It looked as if he had been wrong, suspecting Sid Toner of any underhand game. He decided he'd make up his recent curt treatment of his right-hand man at the first opportunity. As soon as the weekend's operations were over in fact. He looked at the recumbent form beside him. He didn't like whores all that much and this one, a blonde Scandinavian, was no exception. Standing up, she was almost a foot taller than the gang boss, which accounted for the fact that he didn't let her stand up all that often. Even so, he had been having problems recently. At his age impotency was a joke you still made about other men but you kept your fingers crossed, just in case. He dug the girl in the ribs until she opened her eyes.

'Try again,' he commanded.

The girl closed her eyes again and slid down under the sheets to begin what she knew was a hopeless task but which she couldn't afford to refuse.

A few miles away, in his Wimbledon home, Sid Toner was also awake. He was going over everything planned for the next three days until he was sure there were no flaws. Nothing could go wrong, he eventually decided, but he still couldn't get to sleep. It was the split between himself and Reeder that worried him. He still didn't know why the gang boss was being off-hand but there was no doubt about it. It was a trifle worrying. He wondered about the advisability of having a word with his contact when he came back from his holiday in Vienna. Might be an idea to see if he could set up a little operation himself, maybe as an adviser. Not just to Reeder but all the London bosses. A sort of crime consultant. He nodded in satisfaction. It had a nice ring to it—you could almost put it in the yellow pages.

Not all that far from either Sid Toner or Jack Reeder, two very worried BBC television executives were sitting in a darkened room playing over a video-recording of the Michael Parkinson Show due to go out at eleven o'clock on Saturday night, only eight hours away. When it was over they looked at one another in panic-stricken silence. It was worse than they'd imagined, even after hearing reports from the hysterical producer just before he'd been taken to hospital in the same ambulance as the show's unconscious presenter. It was no use thinking about re-making the programme or doing it live with another guest, not with the star displaying two black eyes and a badly cut nose.

'Bloody drunken American band-leading bastard,' one executive muttered.

'He was still drinking when he left here,' the other said. 'God help the poor bastards who have to work with him at that festival.'

CHAPTER TWENTY-FOUR

By six o'clock on Saturday afternoon Lew Jackson was convinced he was going to make a fortune. The afternoon concert was almost over and the fans were having a ball. True, the Town Hall was only about three-quarters full, but there seemed little doubt many of the audience would be taking up available tickets for subsequent concerts and the word would definitely spread. The concert had opened with the Clark Terry Quartet and the problems he'd been having at the previous day's rehearsal in the club had faded. The group had played brilliantly and Terry had been in particularly devastating form. The quartet had been followed by Joe Williams, singing with a trio led by Joe Nealis. After a shaky start, when his mind was clearly on other things, Nealis got everything together and the set went with a real bang.

The second half of the concert opened with the Kenny Davern–Dave McKenna Duo and they had been a knock-out. Davern was on soprano saxophone, an instrument he'd neglected since the break-up of Soprano Summit back at the end of 1978. Today he had left his clarinet in its case and proceeded to blow his bun off. Then, Art Blakey's Jazz Messengers had gone on. At first the band was a shade ragged, then Blakey put in a crashing eight-bar drum break. It wasn't scheduled and, judging from the red-hot glare which Blakey directed from one man to another, it was his way of telling them to get their shit together. They promptly did and now their set was more than half over. Uninterrupted by such non-essentials as spoken introductions, there had been a sustained roar of sound coming off the stage to the huge delight of the fans and the despair of a man in the back row who was counting decibels on a little machine, his ears well stuffed with cotton wool.

Lew, resplendent in a violet and green suit, apparently made from deck-chair material, and black velvet fedora, had introduced each artist. He was standing back-stage with Joe as Blakey thundered away, yanking his Messengers along by the roots of their influences. 'Christ,' Lew said to Joe in the quiet shout necessary to make himself heard. 'The bloody roof'll go off any minute now.'

Almost before his words were out there was a sudden vibration and a little cloud of dust puffed out from beneath the floorboards of the stage.

'If the floor doesn't cave in first,' Joe remarked.

'God help us all when Ray Curtis gets out there tonight,' Lew said with delighted anticipation.

'Speaking of our drunken friend, have you heard anything of him?'

'No, probably still picking pieces of Michael Parkinson out of his fingernails.'

'What is all this about Parkinson?' Joe asked.

Lew told him.

'Rotten bastard,' Joe said.

'Who is?'

'You are.'

'Takes one to know one. Anyway, serves him right.'

On stage the Jazz Messengers thundered to the end of *E.T.A.* and the audience erupted into applause which would have done credit to a crowd twice their size.

A few minutes later the band came off and Lew, Joe and the other performers who had stayed on to hear Blakey gathered round to deliver congratulations. Eventually, when the musicians had gone into their dressing-rooms, Lew turned to Joe and executed a very neat twirl. 'What a knock-out. We're on our way, old son, we're on our way.'

Joe sniffed.

'What's the matter? Jealous? Don't worry, you're not alone. There must be a couple of million aspiring drummers around who would give their back teeth to play like him, even if he is well past sixty.'

'You might be right but it isn't what I was

sniffing at.'

'What were you sniffing at?'

'It's that smell again.'

'What smell?'

'Same as last night. Old houses and something burning.'

'No vinegar this time?'

'Not so far.'

'Probably a frying microphone somewhere.'

Joe shrugged his shoulders, 'Okay, if the place burns down, don't blame me.'

'I won't. Now, we've got two hours before the second concert. I'll get a quick cup of something and a sausage roll while you see Reeder's lads know how to set up the stage. When I get back you can go and eat.'

Joe wandered off, still sniffing. Lew tried an experimental sniff. There was an unusual smell in the air, and Joe's description seemed to fit, but it was nothing to worry about. There were always odd smells in old buildings, particularly those used for public performances. Some of the theatres they'd played in the old days had boasted aromas which could be shredded with a cheese-grater and probably had been.

He went out of the stage door, past a large, shapeless man whom he took to be the individual who'd given them the elbow the night before, and climbed into the Granada. He was pulling away down the alley when something jabbed him in the back and he aged about ten years. He braked hard and screwed a quick glance over his shoulder. It was the Honeydripper's brother, Winston.

'What did you do that for?' Lew demanded. 'Christ, you scared me out of my bloody boots.'

'Sorry, Mr Jackson. I wanted to see you.'

'Have you found her?'

'No.'

'Then what do you want?'

'Dwight said I'd to tell you we keep falling over policemen.'

'I expect you do. They're looking for her as well.'

'He was worried in case we got arrested.'

'You're looking for your sister. That's no crime. If you run into any trouble tell them, and if that doesn't help call this man.' He found a scrap of paper and wrote on it the name of the trombone-playing solicitor who'd held Joe's hand during Blackstone's questioning.

'Right, thank you, Mr Jackson.' Winston opened the rear door and slid out. The door slammed and Lew engaged gear again. As he did so he noticed a small, greyish-white cloud escaping from an air vent down at ground level along the side of the Town Hall. He put the car back into neutral and climbed out. Once he was close to the vent he could hear the sound of an extraction fan and realized the cloud was dust, not smoke. He grinned to himself. He was letting Joe's fantasies about the place burning down get the better of him.

He got back into the car and headed for the club and a quiet drink and, if there was anything edible in the kitchen, something to eat too.

He was sitting in the little office behind the bar, drinking a comparatively weak scotch and chewing a cheese sandwich he'd nailed together from a few scraps he'd found in what passed for the pantry, when someone came clattering down the steps into the club. Lew went out to see who it was. The owner of the noisy feet was a skinny, very young police constable in a uniform which appeared to have been made for someone else.

'Mr Jackson?' the constable asked.

'Yes, that's me. Now what have I done?'

'They told me I would find you here.'

'Who did?'

The policeman consulted a shiny new notebook. 'Casimir Sound Productions of Baker Street.'

'Who? Oh, them, yes, they're the sound engineers at the festival.'

'That may well be,' the young man said portentously. 'However, they assure me that, during the period the goods are on hire, you are responsible for their safe-keeping.'

'Correct, now what. . . .'

'In that case, can you give me a satisfactory explanation why there is a large quantity of packing cases on an open space between Barnes and Putney cemeteries?'

219

'Eh?'

The notebook was consulted again. 'To be precise, thirteen crates, five large and eight small, together with a quantity of shavings and other packing materials.'

Lew stared at the young policeman as if he was out of his mind. 'But they're in the basement,' he said.

'I can assure you they are not in any basement,' Mr Jackson. They are on an open site between Barnes and. . . .'

'All right,' Lew said. 'If you say they're there, then that's where they are.'

'They must be removed. . . .'

'I'll see to it.'

'There are laws, you know. . . .'

'Okay, I'm sorry.'

'My superior officers might wish to take matters. . . .'

'All right,' Lew yelled and then, seeing the affronted gleam in the young man's eye, hastily apologized and eventually managed to persuade him to leave with the assurance he'd deal with the problem as soon as he'd finished his sandwich.

He sat down again in the office and picked up his glass, thought about a refill but decided against it. With Ray Curtis to contend with, a clear head might be an asset. He tried another bite at the cheese sandwich and was in mid-chew when several things came together in his mind.

For a start there was the ever-present awareness that he had been manoeuvred into a position where he had to accept help from Reeder and Toner. There was Reeder's condition that all the help in the hall had to be Reeder's men, and there was the council official who had put the hall at his disposal and was apparently receiving dropsy from Reeder. Then there were funny smells back-stage, vibrations, little clouds of dust and the smell of burning. Now the fact that the basement, which should have been filled with empty crates and packing cases, was apparently empty. Whatever Reeder was up to he was doing it beneath the stage of the Town Hall.

He swallowed the remains of the sandwich and went behind the bar to pour himself another scotch before he remembered he'd decided against it. He sipped at the drink while he thought. There didn't seem to be any logic in it. What could Reeder want in the basement of the Town Hall? Anyway, the most important thing was to see that he didn't mess up the remainder of the festival. That had to go ahead, especially after the afternoon's great start. If the rest of the weekend was as good, then he had it made. It was money in the bank.

He finished his drink and was half-way up the stairs when his thoughts suddenly went into high gear. Money in the bank, was it? Or to be precise, money in two banks, one on each side of

221

the Town Hall and, to pile insult upon insult, one of them was where he kept his overdraft. He almost fell down the stairs in his eagerness to get to the telephone.

He dialled the number of the police station and asked for Blackstone.

'He's not here,' a tinny voice told him.

Lew thought hard. What was the name of the sergeant Blackstone had told him to ask for? Green, that was it. He asked for him.

'There's no Sergeant Green here,' the voice said.

Lew tried again, going so far as to spell the name just in case the voice on the telephone belonged to an idiot.

'We've no Sergeant Green here now and we never have had a Sergeant Green. Of course,' the voice went on, tinnily sarcastic, 'if we ever get one you'll be the first to know.'

Lew spluttered slightly, then banged down the receiver and ran out of the office and up the stairs, moving faster than he'd moved for years. He was well on the way to the Town Hall when he realized, whatever else he might be, he wasn't a hero. He turned off with a screech of nearly bald tyres and headed instead towards the Honeydripper's family home. Her brothers might not be too much of a match for Reeder's heavy mob but if they could round up enough helpers at least they would be an effective barrier between himself and physical violence.

He looked at his watch. Less than an hour to go before the evening concert started. He had very little time left and as praying wasn't his line he tried swearing. After a few minutes he gave it up because it didn't seem to be making him any happier either.

Ten minutes later he had two young West Indians in the back of the Granada, both of whom claimed to be related to Honey and who had believed Lew's hastily concocted tale that Jack Reeder was keeping her locked in the basement of the Town Hall. Now all he had to do was find Dwight, Winston and the others and, more important, think of a story to tell them when they got into the basement and found he'd lied about Honey being there. For once his mind refused to work. It looked as if the evening might very well end with aggravation of a different sort from that which he had been anticipating.

CHAPTER TWENTY-FIVE

George Blackstone was feeling decidedly diminished. He stood in the dressing-room at the Town Hall feeling like a small boy who had been found whizzing a mince pie out of the oven before parental authority had been given. In front of him, her round black face set in a ferocious glare, Big Mama Richards was waiting for an explanation.

'You took my words and put your own meaning on them,' Blackstone said.

'I'd like to believe you,' the black singer told him. 'But I have had a bellyful of trouble over the years, with white cops in particular. I didn't expect it here in London and I certainly didn't expect it from you. Not after you passed those tests.'

'What the hell is all this about tests?' Blackstone demanded.

'My manager died last month,' the singer explained. 'I've had him for thirty years and he knew what to do and when to do it. He could hold his liquor and he could fuck until the sun came up. Now, I've been around a long time but things have never really happened for me. Now they are and I'm all alone. I need someone who can take care of himself and me if the going gets rough.'

Blackstone stared at her as if she had taken leave of her senses. 'Manager. So that's what all this is about. You want me to be your manager. Good God, woman, you're mad.'

'What's wrong with that? I've been looking and you measure up pretty good.' She dropped her glance to his crotch and the first smile he'd seen since the bust-up the previous day edged on to her face. 'Yeah, pretty good.'

'Ridiculous,' Blackstone snorted.

'Why is it?'

'For one thing I don't know how to manage a singer.'

'Neither did my last manager. Fact is, he couldn't manage the hole in his ass but he could do eveything else that was called for.'

'Anyway, I don't like jazz.'

'You don't have to listen.'

'I don't like jazz musicians.'

'You like me, don't you?'

Blackstone stared at her and suddenly realized he did like her—pseudo-tough manner, salty tongue and all. 'Well, yes,' he said reluctantly.

'There, I knew it. Now, this retirement of yours, you can hurry it along, can't you? Take it early.'

'Well, yes, but. . . .'

'No buts, I've got to be back in the States in a week.'

'That's impossible. . . .'

'Well, as soon as you can. Now it's all fixed. Don't worry about money. I'm making enough now to pay you real well.'

'Look. . . .'

'Now, we got to put the seal on this little matter,' Big Mama said, and reached past the policeman to turn the key in the dressing-room lock.

'What did you do that for?'

'Can't you guess?' the singer said as she came

towards Blackstone in a knife-fighter's crouch, her left arm outstretched, fingers threateningly curved.

Blackstone, knowing the mark of a professional when he saw it, moved backwards. 'Keep away,' he warned. 'I am a police officer and I am here on official business.'

'The hell you are, lover.'

'Madam. . . .'

'And cut out that whorehouse talk.'

'I. . . .' Blackstone's spluttering was cut off abruptly when someone rapped loudly on the door.

'What is it?' Big Mama yelled.

'You're on,' an anonymous voice called.

'You bet your ass I'm on,' she shouted back.

'Two minutes,' the voice said, and footsteps retreated along the corridor.

'Shit,' Big Mama said, and rose from her menacing crouch to a height that wasn't much greater. 'Well, what I have in mind is going to take a whole lot longer than two minutes so we'll have to wait.'

Blackstone relaxed visibly.

'But not for long,' Big Mama warned, and reached out playfully to tweak the zip-fastener on his flies.

Blackstone yelped and covered himself with both hands, looking for all the world like a tweed-jacketed, fifteen-stone Venus Arising.

Big Mama unlocked the door and opened it.

'Remember, we haven't finished.' She went out and headed for the stage.

With a strangled gasp of relief the big policeman followed her out and, in his determination to get to safety, didn't notice his thin, dyspeptic sergeant who was standing a few feet away, half hidden by a fire-hose on a large bright red reel.

The sergeant watched him go, his expression mingled with disbelief at what he had heard through the dressing-room door and unconcealed elation at the fact that he had, at last, found a way, however unlikely, of terminating his relationship with his superior officer.

Big Mama Richards was closing the first half of the evening concert. The concert had started well, Harry Betts managing to retain the form he had shown at his last couple of gigs at the South Bank Jazz Club. The rest of the band he was nominally leading—Sammy Allon, Curly Shatner and Joe Nealis—had responded to him and to the enthusiasm of the crowd who had, admittedly, come to hear other artists but had applauded generously. Joe had been a shade miffed at the non-appearance of Lew, which had resulted in him being unable to get anything to eat and had also lumbered him with the chore of introducing Betts and the following act.

His introduction of Big Mama Richards was greeted with an ear-splitting yell of approval from the audience who had become familiar with her singing from a handful of records which had been available for the past year or so, but had never before had the opportunity of hearing her in person. Big Mama was being accompanied by a quartet led by Sammy Allon, whose immediate reappearance on stage was also approved by the crowd, and by a singing group. The group consisted of three tall, thin black girls, each of whom towered over Big Mama. Their silver sheath dresses, split to the thigh, and silver-blonde curly wigs made an odd contrast with the short, fat singer's pale yellow dress which projected outwards and downwards from her shoulders, making her look like a small, mobile haystack.

With a curt nod from the singer, Sammy rolled out the slow opening chords of the verse of *A Good Man Is Hard to Find*. Big Mama's deep, sonorous voice stilled the audience. As she reached the last lines of the verse,

My happiness it never lasts a day,
My heart is almost breaking while I say . . .

her eyes fell on Detective-Chief Superintendent George Blackstone who, unable to resist the chance to hear the fat little woman performing, had used his authority to gain access through the exit close to the stage, unaware that his action had almost brought on a coronary from one of

Reeder's men who was doubling as attendant. At the sight of the policeman Big Mama began the chorus, switching into a faster tempo than expected by Sammy and the rest of the quartet, but they followed without any appreciable hesitation. The words of the tune's chorus were clearly aimed at Blackstone, and he found himself grinning with unexpected pleasure. For several more songs the singer's voice—big, rounded, powerful—echoed through the hall, even when she eschewed the use of the microphone, later in her set, to belt out an up-tempo version of *You've Been A Good Old Wagon*, without benefit of amplification.

By the time she had reached her last number the entire audience was hanging on every nuance of her remarkable voice. For Blackstone it was an astonishing revelation, an experience he hadn't expected. He had enjoyed every moment of it and even had a wide grin plastered across his face. There was no doubt an encore would be required and it was then that Big Mama set the seal on whether or not Lew would get his wish for a flood of late bookings for the rest of the shows which included a further appearance by Big Mama at the Sunday night concert.

'We're going to give you another song,' she told the audience, and waited for the roar of approval to die down. 'This is something we haven't rehearsed,' she went on, surprising

Sammy and the rest of the band, who had prepared for such an eventuality with a fast version of *After You've Gone.* She turned away from the microphone and took a pace towards the piano. 'Play me some blues, lover. Something down real low.' Sammy obliged and Big Mama returned to the microphone, speaking over his playing. 'Maybe you've heard this song but with different words.'

She nodded her head at Sammy who brought in the rest of the group as Big Mama began singing.

I got nipples on my titties, big as the end of my
    thumbs,
I got something between my legs that'll make a
    dead man come,
Oh, baby, baby won't you shave 'em dry.
Won't you grind me baby, grind me 'til I cry.
Say, I've fucked all night, all the night through
    baby
And I feel just like I wanta fuck some more.
Oh, great God, daddy, grind me honey, shave
    'em dry
And when you hear me holler, baby, want you
    to shave 'em dry.

The audience had sat through the opening words in the silence of ever-increasing disbelief. Then, as she began a reprise of the opening lines, they erupted in a deafening roar eclipsing everything that had gone before.

For Blackstone the words had an astonishing effect. He felt himself stirring and reached down with a warning hand to find, to his embarrassment, that Big Mama's earlier grab for his zip had been more effective than he'd believed. There was a gap that shouldn't have been there and, if his reaction to her singing continued, very soon wouldn't be. He turned and hastily let himself out through the fire exit. He went out into the alleyway and adjusted his unzipped flies then stood for a moment, hesitant.

His doubt about what to do next was settled when his sergeant appeared. 'Ah, there you are, sir.'

'What is it?'

'A message for you, sir. The lady said would you see her in her dressing-room immediately after she comes off stage.'

'What? You mean. . . . When did you speak to her?'

'Just as she went on sir, I was standing in the wings. She said it was important, something she'd forgotten to tell you. Something about Jack Reeder.'

'Reeder?'

'Yes, sir,' the sergeant said without a blush.

Blackstone nodded. 'Yes, very well, Green. Er, I think perhaps you'd better come with me.'

The sergeant shook his head decisively.

231

'Afraid not, sir. I had a call from the nick. They have some information that seems relevant. I said I'd go back right away.'

Blackstone nodded. 'Yes, right. You get back while I see er, Miss, er, Richards.'

'Yes, sir.' The sergeant floated off without giving Blackstone a chance to change his mind. Once out of sight of the Chief Superintendent he headed for the pub across the road from the Town Hall. He treated himself to a small gin and tonic and the drink slid down without any apparent effect upon his incipient ulcer. It was going to work, he thought, it was bloody well going to work.

Inside the Town Hall the first half of the concert had ended and the fans were stumbling towards the three bars with thirsts aggravated by the bawdy earthiness of Big Mama's performance. Back-stage there was a solid mass of people as the artists who had finished were falling over those preparing to go on in the second half. In the crush the arrival of Jack Reeder and Sid Toner went unnoticed by anyone except one of their own men who had been allocated the task of keeping a parking space clear for Toner's wife's anonymous Mini.

'Any problems?' Sid asked the man.

'None, Mr Toner. The mob in there are making enough racket to cover a bloody bomb going off.'

'Good, good.'

'Just one thing, Mr Toner.'

'What?'

'We've had the jacks here.'

'What was that?' Reeder demanded.

'The jacks. Blackstone and his sergeant.'

'Jesus Christ Almighty,' Reeder said and started to wriggle his bulk back into the Mini.

'It's all right, Mr Reeder,' the man said. 'He doesn't know anything. He's sniffing around that singer, Big Mama Richards. Keeps going in and out of her dressing-room.'

Toner frowned as Reeder scrambled out of the car again. 'What about the sergeant?'

'He's gone. Anyway he's half asleep all the time.'

'I don't like it, Sid,' Reeder said.

Toner thought for a moment. 'It's a bit of a joke, isn't it, though?'

'A joke?'

'Yes. Old Blackstone up above while we're down below pulling the biggest tickle ever right under his feet.'

Reeder thought about it. 'Well,' he said grudgingly. 'One thing, so long as we know where he is, we have the edge.' He turned to the labourer. 'You say he's in her dressing-room now?'

'Yes, Mr Reeder.'

'Is she in there as well?'

'She was still on stage when I came out but I expect she'll be there now.'

233

Reeder grinned tightly at Sid Toner. 'Tell you what,' he said. 'If he's fancying a bit of the other then let's help him. Make sure they're both in there, Blackstone and this black bird, and no one else. Then fix it so they can't get out. At least not until the end of the concert. By then there'll be nothing for him to hear anyway.'

'Right, Jack,' Toner said, pleased to be again sharing a joke with Reeder, even if it was one that skated on slightly thin ice.

CHAPTER TWENTY-SIX

'Everything okay?' Toner asked, eyeing the neatly arranged explosives with a wary eye.

'All set,' the Welshman told him.

They were in the basement of Lloyd's Bank, where it was clear that the time since Toner's last visit had been well spent. The three charges the big Geordie had exploded during Art Blakey's set on the Saturday afternoon concert had opened the way from the passageways into the main basement of both banks and the jeweller's. Now they were ready for the big bangs. With only ordinary brick walls, the first five charges had been small. The next two, into the banks' vaults, had to penetrate reinforced concrete and a sheet-steel inner lining. They would make a lot of noise.

'You're sure the band will be loud enough?' Reeder asked.

The big Geordie looked at the short, Napoleon-like figure and Sid, intercepting the gleam in the big man's eye, stepped in hastily. 'Very loud band,' he assured Reeder. 'Went right off the scale, didn't they?'

One of the electronic experts nodded his head.

Toner seized on him as a means of changing the subject. 'You're sure the alarm systems have been neutralized?' he said to the man, and immediately regretted it.

'Jesus Christ,' the man snarled at him. 'What the fuck do you think we've been doing in this bloody cellar all this time? Playing with our fucking selves?'

'Just checking,' Toner said hastily.

'Are you staying?' the Welshman asked.

Toner glanced at Reeder and got the expected, imperceptible movement of his boss's head. 'No, we have a lot to do up above,' he replied, trying to make it sound as if they had something important to do and were not merely intent on being well away when the charges were detonated. There was an awkward silence during which Toner and Reeder tried to exercise their authority without saying anything to the men who, although unwilling to speak their thoughts, made it very clear with a few sniffs, coughs and a shuffling of feet that they didn't think much of people who planned raids, then pushed off when the going got a shade tricky.

'What time does the last band go on?' Toner asked eventually, more as a means of breaking the silence than because he wanted to know.

'Eleven,' the Welshman said, glancing at the well-creased handbill. 'As soon as the band on now comes off, which'll be in about ten minutes.'

Reeder looked round for a familiar face. 'Herbie, go up and see that Blackstone's locked away in that woman's dressing-room.'

'Who's Blackstone?' someone asked.

'Somebody we don't want to see just at the moment,' Toner said quickly.

They followed the little man in the boiler suit through to the Town Hall basement and waited as he went up the stairs and disappeared through the door. Moments later he was back, his face wrinkled in a frown.

'What's up?' Toner demanded.

'Not sure, Mr Toner.'

'What the hell does that mean?' Reeder snapped.

'Well, the place is full of people, about thirty of 'em.'

'That's the band, they'll be waiting to go on.'

'Yes, well, seems a lot for one band. That bloke's there, the one who's running this festival, you know, Mr Toner, the one what came out to Eddie Lester's place in Hampstead.'

'Lew Jackson?'

'That's him.'

'What of it?'

'Well, he's up there with half a dozen West Indians.'

'They'll be one of the bands.'

Herbie shook his head. 'No, there's no blackies on tonight. Apart from the singer. The rest of 'em are all white.' He looked a little uneasy. 'I think I recognized one of them. He's a brother of that whore. You know, the one they call the Honeydripper.'

'What the bloody hell are they doing in there?' Reeder hissed angrily at Toner. 'I thought it was clearly understood, no one comes into this place except musicians or our blokes.'

'It'll be all right, Jack,' Toner said quietly. 'We'll just wait until they clear out, then we'll go.' He looked at the ring of faces around him and was irritated to see that several of them bore malicious grins. He glanced at his watch. It was nearly eleven o'clock. The Ray Curtis band would be going on stage any minute now but there was still time for Jack and himself to get clear. The band would be on for at least three-quarters of an hour and there was no need for the Geordie with the tattooed ear lobes to blow the vaults during the first loud number the band played.

He settled himself on one of the steps leading out of the basement and, after a moment, Jack

237

Reeder did the same. 'That bloody Jackson wants sorting out,' Reeder muttered to Toner.

'He's only doing what we want him to do, Jack.'

'Filling the bloody place with West Indians isn't what we wanted him to do.'

'Herbie probably exaggerated. Give it a few minutes and I'll go up and have a look myself.'

Reeder grunted in reply and cast a glare upwards which should have burned holes in the ceiling and incinerated Lew Jackson.

In fact, Lew was feeling decidedly uncomfortable but the unseen glower from Reeder wasn't the cause. He had arrived at the town hall with six young West Indians, all of whom were eager for some action, not entirely a result of their feelings for Honey to whom they all appeared to be related in one way or another. He was sure some of them were interested in a fight for the sake of fighting. They had been confronted at the outer door by one of Reeder's men who had tried to prevent Lew taking his army in with him. The army had surrounded the man and moments later, somewhat bloodied about the nose and decidedly unconscious, the man had been bundled into the back of an adjacent Mini. They had entered through the door and mingled with a solid throng of people. Lew soon spotted another of Reeder's men, this one standing with his back to the cellar door and effectively barring it from casual entry.

Lew wasn't too worried for the moment. The West Indians didn't know which was the door to the cellar and in any event, as he pointed out to them, they would have to wait until the next band went on stage, thus making a little more room for them.

He detailed Dwight as his deputy commander, told him to keep everyone where they were, and then headed towards the wings where he could see Joe Nealis listening to the Scott Hamilton Quartet. As he reached Joe the band finished and he dug his partner in the ribs.

'Oh, there you are,' Joe said. 'What kept you?' There was a touch of acid in his voice and Lew decided to avoid confrontation, something he didn't need at that particular moment.

'We might have a bit of a problem,' he whispered.

'Is that all.'

'A serious one. I think Reeder is up to. . . .'

'Bloody marvellous,' Nealis said to Hamilton as he came off stage.

'Oh, yes, great,' Lew added, trying to sound as if he'd been there all the time.

'Thanks,' the young tenor saxophonist said quietly. 'After the way Big Mama Richards went over I thought we might have a few problems.'

'She was good, was she?' Lew asked, momentarily forgetting he was supposed to have been there like the good festival promoter he was trying to be.

'Good's hardly the word for it,' Joe said. 'Mind you, if the local watch committee were in we might have a few problems.'

'Watch committee? What're you talking about?'

'Later,' Joe said. He nodded at Chuck Riggs, the drummer with Scott Hamilton's group, then whispered to Lew so that Riggs couldn't hear. 'I know what Curtis meant when he said Hamilton was too young. I feel the same way about guys like Riggs. That age and already he's forgotten more about drumming than I've ever known.' He watched the young musicians disappear towards their dressing-rooms and then stepped hastily back as Ray Curtis came into view heading straight for Lew, a fierce expression on his face.

'All set?' Lew said, trying a smile.

'Jesus Christ, what was that stuff you sent me?'

'Chivas Regal,' Lew said innocently.

'Is *that* what it was? Christ, but it was potent. I thought straight scotch was some drink, but boy. . . .' He shook his head. 'Can't say I remember much about the TV recording but it must have been some session.'

'Why?'

Curtis held up his right hand, proudly displaying a set of scraped knuckles.

Lew grinned. 'I'll lay on a crate of it,' he said.

Curtis laughed, something neither Lew or Joe

ever remembered anyone who knew the man mentioning as a normal characteristic. 'Yeah, well. Later.' He glanced on-stage where his band were already assembled. He slipped the guard from the mouthpiece of the alto saxophone he had slung around his neck and moistened the reed. He caught the eye of the band's piano player, who began a fast introduction to *Doodle Oodle*. After eight bars, bass and drums joined in, then the brass section came in with a smash. 'Right,' Curtis said to Lew and Joe. 'Let's show those bastards how a real jazz band sounds.' He stalked out from the wings, playing as he went. By the time he reached centre stage his solo was already developing, building towards the point where the full band would come in behind him.

'You've got to hand it to the bastard,' Lew said to Joe. 'He can play.'

'It doesn't make him less of a bastard, although I have to admit he's been less trouble than I expected.'

'It's because I found the way to his heart,' Lew said, and glanced round to where the West Indians were massed. 'I think I'll be going,' he added. 'It's time I settled a little problem.'

'What problem's that?'

'I think Reeder's going to try to break into the banks next door.'

'Sounds like a good idea. What'll he do for an encore?'

241

'I'm not joking, mate.'

Joe looked at him, and something in Lew's face confirmed that he was serious. 'Oh, sweet Jesus. So that's what he's been up to.'

'Yes, well, it's all under control.'

'You've called the police?'

'Not exactly.'

'What does that mean?'

'I tried but they were out.'

'What do you mean, out?'

'Blackstone wasn't there and they'd never heard of Sergeant Green.'

'They're here somewhere. I saw both of them earlier.'

'Thank Christ. Where are they now?'

'I've no idea.'

'Well, try and find them. I'll go and calm down the lads.'

'What lads?' Joe looked in the direction Lew was facing and saw the West Indians for the first time. 'What the hell are they doing here?'

'They've come to help.'

'Why? Do they fancy their chances against Reeder's professionals?'

'I told them Honey was being held in the basement.'

Joe turned bright pink. 'Honey?'

'Yes, mind you, when they get down there and find she's isn't in the basement, I might have a bit of trouble with them. Still, it's a nicer kind of trouble.' He glanced at Joe. 'If you can find Blackstone quickly, maybe we won't have to go down, although they seem to be getting a bit impatient.'

Joe put his hand on Lew's arm. 'Look, there's something I think I should tell you. . . .'

'Christ,' Lew said, interrupting him. Two of the West Indians had at last realized the significance of the large man in a dress suit who was propped against the cellar door. They had begun to move towards him. Lew started across the intervening space and as he did so the cellar door opened, making the guard turn, momentarily putting his back to the danger he wasn't expecting.

A face peered through the opening and Lew recognized the bland greyness of Sid Toner. He broke step for a moment then, as the two West Indians rushed the guard, he ran forward trying his best not to get too close to any action. He suddenly realized all he had to do was try to lock the cellar door and sit there until the forces of law and order arrived. The idea took root as he saw there was a key in the lock but in that same instant he was overwhelmed by a flurry of arms, legs and bodies as the remaining West Indians joined in the rush to overwhelm the guard. Within seconds, his feet barely on the ground, Lew was carried forward the last few yards and then downwards into the cellar. His voice, raised in a plea to wait, was completely drowned by the shouts of his now unwanted and entirely uncontrollable army.

CHAPTER TWENTY-SEVEN

In the course of a long and relatively honourable career, George Blackstone had been obliged to arrest quite a number of women without the aid of a policewoman. Indeed, policewomen were quite high on his list of faults with the police. A fairly high percentage of those female arrests had necessitated the use of some measure of force on the big man's part and, unlike quite a lot of his colleagues, he had long ago overcome any moral scruples he might once have entertained about using violence against a woman.

'Treat 'em like ladies but only as long as they behave that way,' was his dictum.

Big Mama Richards was not behaving like a lady. Unfortunately, Blackstone wasn't trying to arrest her which somewhat inhibited his technique for preventing further indignities being inflicted upon him. The ineffectual grabs at his crotch that had undignified their first meeting had been replaced by a wildly amorous assault on what felt like every part of his person simultaneously. He was backed up against a table in the dressing-room, the naked light bulbs surrounding the mirror behind him sending waves of additional heat over his collar and down his back. One of Big Mama's solid thighs was wedged between his knees, the other leg, short though it was, coiled around the back of one of his legs like a smoothly plumped-out version of a constricting snake that had somehow managed to get itself inside a nylon stocking. Both of the singer's arms were wrapped around his neck, but from time to time one hand broke loose to flash downwards to make exploratory progress reports on his development.

It was this development which was causing him most discomfort at the moment. His enforced celibacy had left him not merely frustrated but also in some doubt about his potential in that department. True, the earlier skirmishes with Big Mama had suggested all might not be lost. Now there seemed no doubt about it and that was what gave him concern. There didn't seem to be a lot of point in protesting disinterest or lack of enthusiasm when a large and ever-growing part of him was making its presence increasingly more obvious in the front of his trousers.

'Now that's what I call a man,' Big Mama stated in a delighted yell which, to Blackstone, sounded loud enough to be heard in Fulham.

'Quiet,' he hissed, and tried to put a hand over her mouth. The movement was instantly misinterpreted as a first positive reaction to his seduction.

'That's more like it, lover. You give Ruby the lovin' she needs.'

A change of her grip gave Blackstone a chance to reach for the door. It was locked and there was no sign of the key in the lock. 'Where's the key?' he demanded.

'I haven't got it,' Big Mama said, which was perfectly true but completely disbelieved.

'I insist. . . .' Blackstone began, but that was as far as he got. The rotund little woman gave an odd sort of shuffle, dipped her head then, with both hands on the lower part of her dress, flipped it upwards. The yellow, tent-like garment flew up and over her head and continued in a graceful arc, to land on the floor at Blackstone's feet. Without a pause in her movements she unsnapped her bra, which floated earthwards like a twin-parachuted spacecraft. The policeman stared open-mouthed at the massive breasts which, freed of their encumbrances, leaped and bounded like two playful brown puppies. Big Mama moved towards Blackstone and the puppies nestled into his waistline. Staring wide-eyed over her shoulder, he saw the opposite view of the scene in the mirror. The stockings which had covered her legs had begun to slide floorwards as if it was skin-shedding time and, raising his eyes slightly, he was astonished to see that knickers were something she apparently went without for

246

her concert appearances. The two giant-sized globes of her buttocks undulated like larger cousins of her breasts, and any self-control the big policeman might have retained disappeared in a blinding flash of desire. He grabbed her, a roar of lust from him blending in perfect unison with her yell of delight as at last she broke through the traditionally stoical reserve of the British.

The only items of furniture in the room were one small upright chair and one spindly settee, neither of which looked capable of withstanding one quarter of their combined weight. In unspoken mutual agreement they sank slowly down to the bare, hard floor. With the soft bulk of Big Mama between him and it, Blackstone had no complaints and if she found it a trifle rough on her anatomy she gave no indication of her discomfort.

Their coupling was almost instantaneous, mutual desire having removed any need for gentle, lasting foreplay. They bounded and rolled, sweated and groaned and somewhere along the line Blackstone lost his trousers and any remaining shreds of inhibition. With a vigour which surprised him and delighted her he sustained his attack through approximately seven orgasms, at least two of which were his, and even when they fell still and silent, drawing in huge gasps of air to their starved lungs, there was still enough ardour left to enable him to maintain a pronounced physical connection.

It was some time before he managed to speak and when he did it wasn't what she expected to hear. 'What's that noise?' he asked.

'That's my heart, lover.'

'No. Voices. People shouting, yelling.'

'Must be the audience, maybe Ray Curtis is giving them something they want. Speaking of which. . . .' She wriggled out from beneath him, deftly rolled him on to his back and began a variation he had read about in one of those confiscated books which somehow never did find their way into the police station's boiler-room. Within seconds he lost all interest in the sounds he had heard.

The sounds were not in fact the audience yelling their enthusiasm for the Ray Curtis band. True, the concert hall was filled with sound as the band was in cracking form and was satisfying everyone with their musical verve and attack. But the noises Blackstone had heard were the sounds of a different kind of attack. They were coming from far beneath the stamping feet of the audience, far beneath the sweat-covered back of the big policeman as he moaned in delight at Big Mama's ministrations on the dressing-room floor. The sounds came from a fight which was flowing backwards and forwards through the basement passageways of the Town Hall, the adjacent banks and even as far as the jewellers next door to Lloyd's.

It wasn't a fair and gentlemanly fight but it was reasonably evenly matched. There were six West Indians, all eager to fight, and Lew, eager to avoid violence at all costs, on one side. On the other side about a dozen assorted criminals, half of them specialist who, as a general rule, preferred the more gentlemanly aspects of crime which did not require fighting. An exception to this rule was the Geordie with the tattooed ear lobes, who was weighing in with great glee and determination and more than making up for his recalcitrant colleages. As for Jack Reeder and Sid Toner, of them there was no sign whatsoever.

Their absence didn't concern the West Indians who didn't know they had been there anyway. Lew, however, did know that Toner at least was down there and his absence alarmed him. If there was another way out of the cellar system then it could well prove disastrous if the gang bosses got out. For one thing they might return with reinforcements. For another, they might simply decide to go into hiding until all the dust had settled before venturing out to pick up the pieces of their empire and simultaneously spread pieces of Lew Jackson all over South London.

He began to burrow his way through the sprawling, fighting mob, ignoring a yell from Winston demanding to know where his sister was, and edged his way along a passage which appeared to lead westwards from the Town Hall. He cautiously negotiated a bend in the passageway and was intrigued to realize he was very probably directly underneath the bank holding his overdraft.

He came to a halt when he could see what appeared to be a wall with a hole in it. He eased up to the hole, peered through and, in the gleam of a butane gas lantern suspended from the roof of the passage, he could make out what appeared to be a pile of sleeping bags and some boxes and packages. As he looked at them one of the sleeping bags moved. Cautiously he climbed through the hole in the wall. Two steps and he was close enough to touch the moving bag. He gave it a sharp dig and stepped hastily backwards as the bag sat upright with a yelp and the grey-suited shape of Sid Toner appeared.

The two men stared at one another. 'Bloody hell,' Toner said.

'What is it?' the sleeping bag next to him demanded in the tones of Jack Reeder.

'It's Jackson.'

Reeder's head popped out of the opening at the end of the bag. 'What the bleeding hell are you doing down here?' he demanded.

From somewhere inspiration struck Lew. 'I saw the aggro so I came down to help,' he said, carefully avoiding committing himself to either side in the conflict now raging noisily beneath the stage of the Town Hall.

'Good man,' Toner said, accepting what seemed a self-evident fact. After all, it wasn't likely that some dead-beat musician would try to take on the mighty Reeder mob.

'Come on,' Lew said. 'Follow me.' He started back the way he had come, trying desperately to think what to do next. The others followed and all three men were so deeply engrossed in their own problems that none of them noticed a third sleeping bag had developed life. It sat up slowly and the head of the Manchester-based peterman popped out. Carefully he clambered out of the bag and followed the dim, shadowy shapes of the others. So concerned was he to save himself from violence, prison or any other unpleasantness, that he failed to remember that when he had taken refuge in the sleeping bag he had been wearing the ever-present cigarette on his lower lip. It was no longer there. Soon after he had scrambled through the hole in the passage wall the sleeping bag began to smoulder, then it burst into flames. Within seconds the flames were reaching up the wall towards the boxes and packages carefully stacked there by the big Geordie in preparation for blowing through the wall of the bank's vault.

The explosion, when it came, was very loud and very big. Just as Sid Toner had feared, there was rather more explosive than was absolutely necessary. The problem would not have arisen had the Geordie with the tattooed ear lobes been

251

an expert in the true sense. He was an explosives expert, of that there was no doubt—the trouble was he had never before used his expertise in criminal matters. By nothing more than good luck he had used almost precisely the right amount of explosive for the first charges. Now, faced with blowing his way into a steel-lined, reinforced concrete bank vault, he called upon his vast non-criminal expertise. Unfortunately, all his previous experience had been gained blowing hillsides away in the search for gravel, coal and miscellaneous other natural resources.

As everyone was about to discover, blowing hillsides away wasn't quite the same as blowing a bank vault.

CHAPTER TWENTY-EIGHT

Ray Curtis and his Chicago Big Band were romping through a high-powered performance of the old Lester Young–Count Basie tune, *Dickie's Dream*. The band had built up a considerable head of steam on the number as one fine solo followed another. Curtis himself hadn't put a foot wrong all night and the fact that he was almost twice as old as the next oldest member of the band did nothing but urge the younger men on to greater and greater things. Even the young trumpet player whose lip had been sorely tested during the Friday night rehearsal was out to prove he was so good that even Curtis wouldn't want to fire him when they returned to the States and he could ask for a raise. As they swung into the final ensemble passage with the entire band cracking down like one man it seemed to the audience the only thing that could happen next was that the roof would blow off or the floor cave in.

As the band hit the last chord right on the nose it seemed as if both those structural improbabilities had come to pass. The floor vibrated, the walls shook, and although the roof didn't actually move there were those who later swore it did. Ancient chandeliers swayed, their various parts clinking together with a sound like an arthritic waterfall. Above the proscenium arch several plaster cherubs shook off a few more leaves of flaking paint and even bits of their little anatomies. Dust flew everywhere. The band thought the fans were making all this happen, the fans thought it was the band. Fortunately, no one in the hall realized that the cause of it all was a considerable quantity of explosive going off in the immediate vicinity. If they had, there would have been panic, probable loss of life and a great deal of unpleasantness. As it was, everyone stayed where they were, the fans yelling for more earth-shaking music, the band unable to do anything but meet the demands of this astonishingly vociferous audience.

Curtis yelled a couple of words at the rhythm section who started up a tune the band occasionally used but for which they had no charts. Head arrangements were not something Curtis used very often, mainly because the personnel of the band seldom lasted long enough to allow the mutual confidence such things needed. Tonight, however, he knew the band could do no wrong. The tune they were using was *Casey Stew*, a number put together by Al Casey, Rex Stewart and a whole bunch of other musicians for a reunion of the alumni of the old Fletcher Henderson band. It had worked well for them and it proceeded to work well for Curtis's band of youngsters. The band was well into the number, with the saxophones riffing tightly to form a setting for each of the ten brass players to take solos against, when Curtis noticed what was happening in the wings, which was, to say the least, unusual. Particularly by English standards.

As the explosion had torn holes in the walls of the bank's vaults the blast had hurled darkness, dust and confusion into the massed fighting ranks in the basement. First one, then another of the combatants rushed up the stairs to the safety, light and clearer air back-stage. There, in much pleasanter surroundings, they were able to continue beating seven different kinds of hell out of one another.

Because of the number of people involved and the fact that back-stage at the Town Hall was a trifle restricted for such activities it was inevitable that some of the fighting would get dangerously close to the stage. As Curtis's eyes riveted on what was happening so, one by one, the members of the band followed his eyes until almost all of them were playing with their eyes at right-angles to the direction of their audience.

Soon the audience too became aware that all was not quite as it should be. Of course no one could hear anything over the roar of the band, but the people on the first couple of rows saw occasional glimpses of punches being thrown and feet being raised. Whispered word spread slowly backwards although the story, when it eventually reached the back rows, was very far from the truth.

Any lingering doubts about what was happening were soon dispelled and it was all down to Herbie who, boiler suit shredded by Winston who had taken exception to something the little man had called him in the heat of battle, was having a considerable impression made on his face. Herbie fell over backwards and his outstretched hands caught at and held on to a rope which came adrift from where it had been tied and under his weight began to move. Moments later the entire backdrop, which had concealed an incongruous group of more plaster cherubs, part of the original design of the building which had managed to avoid removal during various refurbishments, sank slowly to the ground.

To the astonishment of the audience this revealed not the usual back-stage scene of bored stage-hands playing cards or even having an illegal smoke. What it revealed was a struggling, battling group of men, all dust-covered to the extent that it was impossible to make out who was who or indeed who were white and who were West Indian. Freed from the restraints of the back-drop the fighters spilled out on to the stage, the first pair sending the music stands of half the trumpet section crashing over. As they were playing a head arrangement it didn't much matter, but when someone else stumbled into the band's drummer, sending his Chinese crash cymbal on to the floor, it was too much for the musician. Chinese crash cymbals are hard to come by and he didn't much relish someone treating his with such disdain. Without missing a beat he reached out and rapped the guilty man across the nose with one of his drumsticks. The man had been about to flatten his opponent, the Honeydripper's brother, Dwight who turned gratefully to the drummer and grinned widely to show his appreciation. As he did so he realized he was now in full view of the audience. Knowing he might never have another chance like it again, he lost all interest in the fight and joined in with the music, playing one of the drummer's tom-toms with his hands the way he played the conga drum.

By this time the fighting was reaching down towards the front of the band where Ray Curtis was standing. Three figures staggered towards him, all dust-covered, one of them short and stout, another seemingly grey and colourless even beneath the layer of dust, the third a vaguely familiar figure who lurched towards Curtis, wiped some of the dust from his face and grinned at the bandleader.

'I'll bet this beats the punch-up on the Parkinson Show,' Lew yelled.

'What the hell is going on?' Curtis yelled back.

'A bank robbery, next door.'

'A bank ... you mean these guys are criminals?'

'Only some of them.'

'Christ, I haven't had a legitimate fight in years,' Curtis said—he unshipped his alto, planted it on its stand and walked forward throwing punches which were as wild and powerful as the playing of his band. The first person he hit was Sid Toner, the second Jack Reeder, and the third was the man his drummer had struck on the nose and who was stumbling amongst the saxophone section trying to find something with which to stem the flow of blood. Being hit by the bandleader was the final straw for the man with the bloody nose and he belted

Curtis squarely in the mouth, thus removing any chance of him playing any encores that night. Such sacrilege was too much for the bemused fans in the front rows. As a man they rushed forward and began trying to scramble up to join in. With a limited amount of space available on stage a considerable amount of jostling took place and soon the fans from the first row were battling with the fans from the second row. The fans in the rows further back and those in the balcony yelled louder than ever, partly because they wanted to hear the band, who had started to lose some of their togetherness, and partly because they couldn't get a share in the action themselves.

Any doubts about the outcome of the battle ended with the intervention of the fans because, apart from fighting amongst themselves, their weight was thrown on the side of Ray Curtis which was on the side of Lew and the West Indians.

Seeing the way things were going, Lew began to edge out of the immediate area of conflict and on his way noticed that Sid Toner and Jack Reeder had disappeared. He looked round for them and was just in time to see Ray Curtis's lead trumpet player surreptitiously revenging himself on his boss's unfair treatment by banging him over the head with a harmon mute.

Lew reached the stage door in time to see a Mini reverse wildly down the alleyway towards the main road with Sid Toner at the wheel. He turned and went back inside.

As he passed one of the dressing-rooms he heard a furious banging from inside. He tried the door, then turned the key which protruded from the lock. When he opened the door he saw that the origin of the sound was a pair of heels banging furiously against the floor. He moved his eyes from the heels along the short, dumpy legs to which they belonged to the large shape of a man who appeared to be wearing a tweed sports jacket and very little else. It didn't take a genius to work out what was happening and he gulped a hasty apology, backed out and closed the door. He stood for a moment, as something familiar about the two figures snatched at his mind. He opened the door again just as the upper figure rolled sideways off the lower one, and Lew found himself staring into two pairs of eyes, both glazed and satiated.

'Well, hello, lover,' Big Mama said. 'I don't know what you want but whatever it is I ain't got none of it left.'

'Beat it, Jackson,' Blackstone rumbled.

'I've been looking for you,' Lew told him.

'I said beat it.'

'There's been. . . .'

'Hop it,' roared the big policeman.

Lew backed out hastily, closed the door and headed for the stage where things were getting even noisier. Someone had run out the fire-hose from the wall close to Big Mama's dressing-room and a jet of water was sending sheet music, instruments and quite a few battered and bruised individuals skating all over the place. By this time all the house lights were up and he gazed out over the milling throng of fans, who were uncertain whether to go home or stay on in case there was more excitement to come. At that moment the main exit doors at the front of the building opened.

Framed in the doorway was the tall, thin figure of the detective-sergeant who had come across the road from the pub to see what all the noise was about. He stood, open-mouthed, at the sight that met his eyes. Then, slowly, he began to make his way forward, not knowing what it was he was going into but aware that whatever it was, and whether he was drunk or sober, tonight was the night he could make a name for himself and get out forever from under the shadow of Detective-Chief Superintendent George Blackstone.

CHAPTER TWENTY-NINE

In the event the detective-sergeant made seventeen arrests, of which thirteen were members of the Reeder mob, two were fans whose enthusiasm for the fray had led them into a part of the Town Hall from which they couldn't get out fast enough, one of Lew's West Indian army who hadn't responded to the sudden call for a victorious withdrawal, and the guitarist from the Ray Curtis Big Band who had become uncontrollably violent when someone stepped on his brand new Ibanez.

The only people he missed were Sid Toner and Jack Reeder, which wasn't very satisfactory but couldn't be helped. In the case of Reeder it was merely a matter of time. Bert Dixon, the scrap-yard owner, had been talking nonstop since he had been found through Lew's efforts with his daughter. The sergeant didn't expect Reg and Alfie to stand up very long when confronted with his testimony, and although Reeder would try his hardest, this time he was for it. The sergeant sent patrol cars along to Reeder's house and to the Wimbledon home of Sid Toner as a precaution, then took a wander through the back-stage area of the Town Hall, savouring the scene of a triumph that should take him at least two jumps up the professional ladder. Always assuming that his little duplicity with Blackstone went according to plan.

A fleet of police cars had arrived to ferry away the prisoners, and Lew and Joe were standing back-stage watching the detective-sergeant and trying to decide whether to laugh or cry when the door to Big Mama Richards's dressing-room opened and first the singer, then Blackstone appeared. The sight didn't surprise Lew, who'd seen them at it, or the sergeant, who'd inveigled his superior officer in there, but it did come as something of a shock to Joe.

'What have they been up to?' he asked Lew.

'It's a long story,' Lew said.

Big Mama heard him. 'It ain't just the story that's long,' she told him.

Blackstone glanced around him at the handcuffed prisoners and the uniformed constables without any apparent surprise or interest. 'Everything under control, Green?' he asked.

'Yes, sir,' the sergeant, whose name wasn't Green, told him.

'Good. Carry on.' Blackstone turned away and, taking Big Mama firmly by the arm, marched towards the stage door.

'Will you be in later to book them?' his sergeant called.

Blackstone stopped and turned round. 'No, you deal with it, Green. They're your arrests and you'll want the credit and you'll have to follow it through. I won't be around long enough.'

'Going somewhere, sir?'

Blackstone glanced down at the little fat singer. 'I'm taking early retirement,' he said. 'I'm going to America.'

Lew watched as the incongruous couple went through the door. 'Was that what I thought it was?' he asked.

The sergeant nodded, a glow of triumph spreading through him. 'That's precisely what it was,' he said.

'Will someone tell me what's going on?' Joe asked plaintively.

'Like I said, it's a long story,' Lew told him. He glanced around him. 'I think I'll make sure Honey's brothers aren't hanging about outside. I have to think of a story to explain why she wasn't in the basement.'

Joe's face pinkened. 'About Honey....' he began.

Just then the door of another dressing-room opened and a curly, silver-blonde popped out. 'Hey, will someone come and do something about this guy in here?'

'Who the hell is that?' Lew asked.

'She's one of Big Mama's backing group, the Silver Belles.'

'The Silver ... I don't remember hiring a backing group for her.'

'I hired them,' Joe said. 'In fact, I suggested to her that it....'

'Hey, are you coming to help?' the girl yelled again.

Lew went in through the door. The other two girls were sitting on a recumbent form which Lew immediately recognized as Jack Reeder. 'What's he doing in here?' he asked.

'He came in while we were changing.

Goddam peeping tom,' the girl who had opened the door said. Lew looked from one to another of them. All three still had on their silver wigs but only one was still dressed in her silver gown. The others were very nearly naked and Lew stared at one of them, seeing something vaguely familiar about the long, thin legs and the tiny breasts.

'Hello, Lew,' the Honeydripper said.

'Honey?' He turned to Joe. 'You knew where she was all the time.'

'Not all the time. I took her home, like I said. When the police went round to my place she saw them coming and hopped through the window. She came back again and told me she'd got a couple of her friends to form a group with her and would I get them a try-out somewhere. It seemed like a good idea to try them here so I spoke to Big Mama and that's it.'

'Mr Jackson, I want a word with you.' Lew turned at the interruption. He recognized the rabbity council official who had been in Reeder's pay. 'This is disgraceful, fighting on council property this way. I won't have it, I am calling a meeting tomorrow to have the rest of the festival cancelled.'

'Oh, no you won't.'

'I assure you I will.'

'If you do I'll tell them you've been in Reeder's pay for years.'

The man turned white. 'You wouldn't dare.'

264

Lew grinned. 'Wouldn't I?' He pointed, and the man looked down at Reeder who was beginning to stir, a faint moan coming from his lips.

The official went even whiter and backed away. 'Well, just be warned. If tonight's activities are repeated. . . .' He turned and ran.

Lew went to the door of the room, stuck his head out and yelled for the detective-sergeant. When the sergeant had happily handcuffed Jack Reeder he grinned at Lew. 'That's the lot.'

'What about Sid Toner?'

'We've got him. I sent a man round to his house. He'd just got there, all covered in dust and claiming he'd been out for a midnight drive. Trouble was there was a body in the back seat of the car he was driving.'

'A body,' Lew said tightly. He hadn't thought the West Indians had hit the doorman that hard.

'Not dead, just unconscious. One of Reeder's men who I'd seen here earlier, so that ruined any chance of Toner cracking on he wasn't here.'

After the sergeant had led away the still-dazed gang boss Lew looked at the Honeydripper and Joe, who were wearing expressions Lew couldn't at first identify. 'Want a lift?' he asked.

Joe and the girl shook their heads without looking at him.

Lew shrugged. 'Okay, suit yourselves.'

'Lew,' Honey said.

'What?'

'I'm sorry.'

'For what?'

'For ... well, for helping set you up with Eddie Lester. I didn't know why, honest. I thought it was to help you.'

He nodded. 'Sure, no harm done.' He grinned at her and Joe. Then a thought struck him. 'What about the blood in your flat. Where did it come from?'

Honey managed to look embarrassed, something he'd never known before. 'I cut myself shaving,' she said.

Lew glanced down at her legs and she shifted uncomfortably. 'Not there,' she said. He raised an eyebrow and she began to giggle. 'Joe asked me to,' she added.

'You dirty old man,' Lew said. 'You'll be asking her to marry you next.'

'I already have,' Joe said.

'What? Bloody hell, mate, that was a joke.'

'Not to me. I'm divorcing Chris and marrying Honey.'

Lew stared at Nealis in silence for a moment. 'There's nothing else you're planning on doing, is there?' he asked.

Joe nodded. 'I'm thinking of going into the agency business. The Silver Belles will be my first act.' He looked suddenly embarrassed. 'For a while anyway. We'll have to change the group when the baby comes. Honey's pregnant.'

266

'Pregnant?'

Honey's expression reflected Joe's embarrassment. 'I didn't believe it myself. It was quite a shock.'

'I'll bet it was.'

'That's why Honey didn't tell her brothers where she was,' Joe put in. 'They accepted her ... working with people like you and me, but coming to live with me was pushing it. If ... when they find she's pregnant they might take a dim view of it. We're not sure how we're going to deal with them.'

'I don't see the problem,' Lew said.

'We're white, Lew, you and me.'

'So what?'

'That's what I say, but Honey seems to think her brothers might be a bit less open-minded.'

Lew shook his head slowly. 'It's a funny old world out there,' he said. He was silent for a moment. 'What about the club?' he asked.

'I don't know, Lew,' Joe said. 'For a while there I thought we might be on our way back to the big time, but now....'

'We are on our way.'

'You might be, but I'm not sure I could stand the strain.'

'There won't be a bank robbery with every concert, you know.'

'Maybe not, but it's still late nights, bad food, too many hassles, too much booze.'

'You think running an agency will be an easy

life?'

'No.'

'Then why make the change?'

Joe's face was serious. 'I think the partnership's run its course, Lew.' He glanced at Honey, who had moved away to talk to another of the Silver Belles, and lowered his voice. 'Anyway, I don't think that's the kind of life I want, not with a kid to bring up.'

Lew shook his head. 'Christ, mate. You a father, at your age, and Honey a mother. What's the world coming to?'

Joe stared hard, opened his mouth to speak then changed his mind and turned and walked towards the door.

The Honeydripper started to follow, then turned and rested her hand on Lew's arm. 'You're not mad about Joe and me, are you?'

'Why should I be?'

'The baby and all that.'

'What's it got to do with me?' he asked. The girl looked at him without speaking and he swore softly under his breath. 'You're not trying to say it's mine?'

'I think so.'

'Christ, Honey, come off it. You're not telling me you know whose it is?'

'That's not a nice thing to say.'

'Well, how can you be sure?'

'I just am, that's all.'

'What does Joe think?'

'He knows it isn't his.'

Lew shook his head slowly. 'I think you're both crazy,' he said.

The girl turned and followed Joe out through the stage door. After a moment Lew walked out into the alley and climbed into the Granada. He sat for a moment. He didn't believe the Honeydripper had any idea who was the baby's father, he wasn't even convinced there was a baby. He tried to understand Joe's motives in doing what he planned, then gave up trying. Even after thirty years he didn't know him any better than he knew himself. He started the engine and drove out of the alley.

Half an hour later he was in the office behind the bar at the club, wondering why he didn't regret Joe's decision to pack things in. Maybe it was for the best, he thought, like Joe had said, perhaps events had run their course.

The telephone rang. It was a man from the BBC asking if Lew would be interested in interviewing Ray Curtis on a weekly arts programme, the interview to be filmed the following day.

'Of course,' Lew said. 'He'll have a cut lip, but I don't suppose it will matter.' There was a muffled sigh from the other end of the telephone. 'No, in certain quarters it would be regarded as satisfactory.'

Lew replaced the telephone and leaned back in the chair. An interview on television, not

269

giving one, which would have been a big step forward, but actually conducting it. It was a leap forward.

The telephone rang again. For a moment he didn't recognize the voice. 'It's Ronnie,' the voice said.

'Ronnie who?'

'Not him, Ronnie Scott.'

'Christ,' Lew said. 'I thought you were dead.'

'I wish I was, but Pete's behind me twisting my arm so I've no choice, I've got to do it.

'Do what?'

'Offer you a two-week stint down here, last two weeks in October.'

'Me?'

'Well, your resurrection hasn't gone entirely unnoticed up here. After all, there aren't many has-beens in our game who wind up promoting festivals. Even if it is in Putney.'

'Jealous?'

'Is that a joke?'

'Can't you tell, you're supposed to be an expert.'

'Well, what about it? Here, don't raise my hopes, you haven't lost your voice have you?'

'No chance. Right, you're on.'

A soft groan came from the other end of the telephone. 'Oh, bloody hell, I thought you'd say that.' There was a click and the line went dead. Lew stared at the instrument, then slowly replaced it. Two telephone calls, two jobs. One on television, the other at Ronnie Scott's. He decided to go home just in case the telephone rang again and someone woke him up.

He went up the stairs of the club and stopped at the top to look over the rail at the scene he'd looked at more times than he cared to remember. Standing there, he decided not to close the club yet. After all, one television job, one gig at Ronnie Scott's and one successful jazz festival wasn't a guarantee the future would be rosy.

He went home to the flat and went to sleep. He woke up again about two hours later and stared into the darkness. What the bloody hell was the matter with him, he thought. Of course the future was going to be rosy. Bloody rosy. He was on his way.

EPILOGUE

A long way from London, in a very good hotel in Vienna, a man sat in his suite sipping a final glass of champagne before joining his wife who was already asleep, the subdued light reflecting from her hair as it spread across the pillow. He smiled gently at her.

He glanced at his watch. The job would be well under way by now, always supposing Jack Reeder and Sid Toner hadn't made a muck-up of it. That was always a possibility when the hands and feet were not of the same calibre as the brain which had created a scheme. He sighed. It had been a very pleasant evening. A particularly fine performance of the Mozart A Major Clarinet Quintet, the centrepiece of a tranquil pool of Haydn String Quartets. So much better than the rowdiness that would be permeating the air of Putney. He shuddered delicately and finished the glass of champagne. Jazz, he thought, was really not for gentlemen.

He climbed into bed and lay staring at the ceiling for a while before turning out the light. Within less than a minute, Jumbo Patel was as sound asleep as his wife.

Photoset, printed and bound in Great Britain by REDWOOD BURN LIMITED, Trowbridge, Wiltshire